BLOODCOUNT

BILL BRAMPTON

THE KENSAL PRESS

British Library Cataloguing in Publication Data.

Brampton, Bill
  Bloodcount
  I. Title
  823'.914 F   PR6052.R268/

  ISBN 0-946041-54-7

Published by The Kensal Press.
Kensal House, Abbotsbrook, Bourne End, Buckinghamshire.

Printed and bound in Great Britain by
Robert Hartnoll (1985) Ltd., Bodmin, Cornwall

To Ghislaine

CHAPTER ONE

Being woken three hours after falling asleep was acceptable. At two hours it was bearable. Between thirty and ninety minutes was the worst. It was just after two o'clock on Friday morning, February 15th, the day after St. Valentine's Day. Stephen had been asleep for forty minutes when his bleeper sounded. His hand shot out automatically towards the alarm-clock and sent his glasses flying to the floor. He groped for the light-switch. He screwed up his eyes against the glare and glanced at the unfocused white shape hanging from the hook on the door. He had left his bleeper in one of the coat-pockets and had no choice but to let the insistent high-pitched pips continue while he picked up the telephone and dialled the switchboard.

'Dr. Hobbs here', he croaked.

'Cardiac arrest. Third floor toilets. Doctors' residence.' He jumped out of bed, got down on all fours and found his glasses. He stood up and rocked back on to the bed to pull his socks on. Shaking and nauseated he got up again and drew his trousers over the Y-fronts he had been sleeping in. At the same time as he stretched into his already buttoned shirt, he manoeuvred his feet into his slip-on shoes – a technique perfected by three years' working as a junior hospital doctor. He grabbed his white coat, stifled the bleeper clipped to the top pocket and rushed out of the room. He was in the corridor with the door shut behind him, before he realised he had left the key inside. As he ran downstairs he swore at the thought that he would later have to go to the porters' lodge to fetch a duplicate key before he would be able to get back into bed.

It was not until the cold air of the hospital court slapped him in the face that he remembered he should not be running towards the main wards.

Muttering profanities and doubting he had heard the switchboard operator correctly, he rushed back into the lobby of the doctors' residence. He banged the lift button, but unusually for that time of night the lift showed no signs of coming. He decided not to wait and took to the stairs. It was now five minutes since his bleep went off. He fully expected to be met by Dr. Reg Dicks, the anaesthetics and resuscitation registrar, who was always the first at the scene of an arrest. But for once Stephen arrived first.

The third floor lavatory looked empty. The only noises were the hissing and dripping of the urinal and the echo of Stephen's feet on the cold stone floor. He was beginning to wonder who was the likely practical joker, when he noticed that the door of the fourth and last cubicle was shut. Through the window above the door filtered the dim light of a standard hospital-issue forty watt bulb. Sheepishly he asked whether anyone was there. There was no reply. He pushed the door but it was locked. With one foot on a radiator and the other on the doorknob he hauled himself up to look through the window. Curled round one side of the lavatory bowl with trousers and pants down to the knees and an arm crooked over the seat lay a body. Stephen let himself down, took a few steps backwards and unsuccessfully shoulder-charged the door.

'You've obviously been watching too many movies, doctor.'

Dr. Reg Dicks had arrived.

'It might help if we could see what we're doing,' said Reg as he switched on the main light and wheeled in his resuscitation trolley.

'There's someone behind the door and it's locked,' replied Stephen superfluously.

'In that case we'd better get the bastard out, hadn't we, doctor?'

As used by Reg Dicks the word 'doctor' was a term of contempt. His quiet clipped voice matched the precise and noiseless way he did everything. Never at a loss what to do he set to work with a pair of forceps and before long he slid back the engaged-vacant bolt from the outside. The door could only open a short way; the feet of the body were wedged against it. Stephen squeezed into the cubicle, lifted the legs away from the inside of the door and pulled the body into the main part of the lavatory.

'Oh God, I don't believe it,' said Stephen.

'Who is it?'

'It's Henry Price . . . I was only talking to him three hours ago.'

There was no sign of spontaneous breathing and no pulse in the neck.

The lips were blue and the face grey but the skin was not yet cold. Whether his heart or his breathing had stopped first was impossible to tell. After a single sharp blow over the heart Stephen began to press the chest forcefully and regularly with the heel of his palm. Meanwhile Reg Dicks extended the neck, pulled the jaw forward and slipped an airway between the teeth and through the larynx into the trachea. As he compressed the rubber bag connected to the airway, the air entering the lungs could be seen to inflate the chest. After thirty seconds Reg took over the cardiac compression while Stephen inserted an intravenous line into the arm and squeezed a bag of bicarbonate into the lifeless body. The ECG monitor showed a straight line interrupted regularly by an upward deflection each time the chest was depressed.

'Are you getting anything?' asked Stephen.

'Absolutely nothing.'

The anaesthetist's competence was of the kind that made him disliked throughout the hospital. Reg the Resuscitator – or 'Resus Reggie' as he was known among the junior hospital doctors – was never wrong. He always knew what he was doing and made sure that everyone else knew it too.

'Thank God, we're getting something now . . .' said Stephen with relief as a few waves of spontaneous cardiac activity rippled across the monitor.

But Reg's attention was elsewhere.

'What have we got here?' he said pulling back the clenched fingers of Henry Price's fist and revealing a used syringe and two empty vials. The vials rolled twards Stephen. He picked them up and read the labels.

'Insulin!'

Before Stephen had completed eight more cardiac compressions, Reg had handed him a syringe loaded with fifty per cent dextrose. He squirted it into the vein through the intravenous line but nothing happened, and the monitor was once again blank.

They continued working on him for thirty minutes. By now a small crowd of spectators had gathered in the doorway. 'Resus Reggie' tried all the tricks in his trolley to bring Henry round. Finally, when an injection of adrenaline through the chest wall directly into the heart failed to produce even the smallest of flickers on the ECG monitor, he announced that there was no point continuing and started to pack up his resuscitatory paraphernalia.

'That's it, folks, Party's over,' Reg told the onlookers. 'You can all crawl back to where you came from.'

He turned to Stephen.

'Who did you say the bastard was?'

'Henry Price . . . the senior registrar on the Rheumatology Unit.'

'Senior registrar? He looks far too old. How old was he?'

'I'm not sure. Early forties I think.'

'I get the picture. A time-expired senior registrar who couldn't get a consultancy. Well, his time's certainly expired now.'

Stephen had always liked Henry Price but he was surprised by the strength of his emotions. He could not stop one of his legs and both his arms shaking. Tears welled in his eyes and he felt a pressure the size of a golf ball at the top of his gullet. When he noticed that Reg was smiling, a wave of anger surged over him but he was too confused to conjure up the perfect phrase to silence the anaesthetist's thoughtless flow.

'Bloody inconsiderate if you ask me,' Reg continued. 'Why the hell couldn't he have chosen the daytime to top himself? Henry Price . . . Yes . . . I know who you mean.'

He had good reason to remember Dr. Price. The dead man was one of the few people ever to make him appear ridiculous. It had happened two months ago. A collapsed man of sixty had been rushed from a restaurant to the Casualty Department. Reg had taken charge as usual and was about to embark on his standard resuscitation routine.

'May I suggest laryngoscopy?' Henry Price said as Reg was preparing to give a D.C. shock to the man's chest.

'And what the blazes do you expect me to find down there, doctor?'

'Boeuf bourgignon, fillet steak or perhaps even a king prawn.'

Reg realised immediately that Henry was almost certainly right. This was a so-called 'café coronary' and the collapsed man had probably inhaled a bolus of food which had partially obstructed the larynx. The story of his discomfiture, when he laryngoscoped the man and removed a large lump of unchewed meat, circulated rapidly among the junior medical staff and was told and retold with relish. Stephen remembered well how the flush of embarrassed fury on Reg's sallow cheeks had matched the return of pinkness to the patient's face.

Reg Dicks turned to leave.

'It will be a coroner's case so you'd better leave everything as it is and call the police. Think you can manage that, doctor?'

Stephen was just about to pull out the intravenous line when Reg stopped him.

'I said leave everything as it is . . . including the I.V.'

*   *   *

Having called the police, it occurred to Stephen that perhaps he had better call the professor. As a junior doctor at St. Nathaniel's he had been brought up to regard the consultant's sleep as sacrosanct and never to be disturbed. It was nearly as bad to wake a senior registrar. Henry Price had been exceptional, the only senior registrar who slept in the hospital on duty nights. His peers went home to Fulham, Clapham or Camden Town, and their juniors were made to feel distinctly inadequate if they rang in the night. The first lesson after qualifying was how to simulate coping with every situation and bluff your way with other doctors, nurses and patients. So engrained in Stephen was this medical macho that he found himself having to debate whether Henry's death was an event of sufficient moment to justify the professorial slumbers being disturbed. His instinct won through. He dialled the hospital switchboard and asked to be put through to Professor Carling's home number. After a few clicks he heard the ringing tone at the other end. Several rings later a woman's faint voice answered.

'Hallo. Who is it?'

'I'm very sorry to disturb you but this is Dr. Hobbs at St. Nathaniel's. I need to speak to Professor Carling urgently.'

'He's not here.'

'Could you tell me where I could reach him, please?'

'He's at the department.'

'You mean in the hospital?'

'Well, that's what he said . . .'

'Thankyou very much. I'm sorry to have had to disturb you.'

The telephone went dead before he had finished his apologies. He dialled the switchboard again and was put through to the professor's office in the Department of Rheumatology. He found it hard to believe that Carling would be in the hospital at that hour but his call was answered after only one ring.

'Who is it?'

'I'm sorry to trouble you, Professor. It's Stephen Hobbs here.'

'What's the problem?'

'Something terrible's happened to Henry Price.'

Stephen heard the professor breathe in deeply.

'He's been found dead. In the doctor's residence.'

'What happened?'

'We tried everything – calcium, adrenaline, fifty per cent dextrose . . .'

'Fifty per cent dextrose?'

'He had some vials of insulin on him and he was holding a used syringe.'

'Christ! What have you done about it?'

'I've rung the police but not the next of kin. I didn't know where to ring.'

'Leave that to me. I'll deal with it. I'll be with you in fifteen minutes.'

Relieved that he would not have to break the news to Henry's family, Stephen returned to the third floor of the doctors' residence. The police were already there. He began to tell his version of events to an extremely young-looking police constable who took down what he said in laborious longhand. He found it hard to suppress a slight annoyance that someone so green was considered adequate to investigate Henry Price's death. But then surely a similar annoyance was felt by some patients when confronted by his own callow looks, freckled face and untameable blond curls.

Stephen described how Henry had been lying in the cubicle and how the syringe and insulin vials were found in his fist. The oddest detail he could remember was how Henry's white coat was hanging neatly on the hook inside the cubicle door. He presumed the police had taken it since it was no longer there.

'Did you know Dr. Price well?' asked the constable.

'I've worked with him for six months but I couldn't really say I knew him well. In fact, I don't know that anyone at the hospital knew him well.'

'Why was that?'

'He was a very private sort of person.'

'You mean unfriendly and difficult to get on with?'

'No. He was very easy to work with. He just wasn't the sort of person who told you his life-story as soon as you met him.'

'How long had he been depressed?'

It was clear that the police had already decided that Henry had killed himself.

'As far as I'm concerned he wasn't depressed,' replied Stephen irritated at the assumption. 'Who told you he was?'

'Was his work going well?'

'What do you mean?'

'Did he enjoy his work?' The constable rephrased the question as though he was dealing with a perverse child.

'He got on well with patients and knew his stuff backwards.'

'But was he getting on in his career?'

'If you mean in terms of promotion, no.'

'He was in a rut professionally, was he?'

'In a sense.'

'In what sense?'

'He was stuck on the career ladder and couldn't get a consultancy.'

'Why not? Wasn't he any good?'

Stephen knew that no useful purpose could be served by losing his temper, but he could not suppress a note of anger in his voice.

'I know it may seem rather strange to you, but Dr. Price's problem was that he was too good. Too conscientious. He spent too much time with patients and too little in research and promoting his career.'

'So he kept on being passed over for more senior jobs?'

'Yes.'

'He had good reason to be depressed then?'

'Disappointed . . . yes. But I can't see Henry Price committing suicide simply because . . .'

'You mean from the little you knew about him?'

'It just doesn't add up.'

At that moment Professor Carling appeared. Because of his great height he was able to sweep past Stephen as though he wasn't there. He took the police constable by the arm and propelled him across to the other side of the room. They spoke too quietly to be heard but Carling was doing virtually all the talking. Stephen waited awkwardly in the doorway. After three minutes there was no sign that his presence was any longer required and he left the room.

It was by now seven o'clock and he remembered that he was locked out of his on-call room. He crossed the court towards the porters' lodge just inside the main gate. It was still dark but birds had begun to chirp in the branches of the ancient trees which formed an avenue in the centre of the court. The bitter cold was as welcome as a cold plunge after a sauna.

11

It helped Stephen to think more clearly. Of course Henry Price could not have killed himself. It was unthinkable. The fountain in the centre of the court tinkled happily as though all the tragedies that occurred each day within St. Nathaniel's were mere punctuation marks in the passage of time.

No one was sitting at the enquiry hatch of the porters' lodge. At the other end of the dingy yellow-walled room were two porters sitting with their feet up on a red formica-topped table. On the table were several cups and an ashtray overflowing with fag-ends. Both porters had newspapers. One was asleep with a copy of the 'Sun' opened out over his torso. The other was reading the sports page. Behind them a small black and white television was indistinctly transmitting the inanities of breakfast TV.

'Excuse me,' said Stephen poking his head through the hatch, 'I'm afraid I've locked myself out.'

The porter was was awake looked up from his newspaper and across at his colleague.

'It's room number twenty-four . . . I wondered if I could have the duplicate key, please.'

The porter looked at Stephen as though he was asking for an interest-free loan.

'I need to get back into the room.'

The porter folded his paper and placed it on the table. He stared at Stephen for several seconds and then heaved his legs off the table. As if he were doing a great and quite undeserved favour he leant back in his chair and took a key from the rows of hooks on the wall behind him. He tossed the key onto the table and started to read his paper again. Stephen opened the door of the porters' lodge, walked to the table and picked up the key.

'You've got to sign for it,' the porter said without looking up.

'Where?'

'In the book.'

Stephen looked round the room and alighted on a book attached by string to a shelf by the enquiry hatch. He opened the book and wrote his name, room number, the date and the time in the appropriate columns. He left the porters' lodge and crossed the court to the doctors' residence.

There was no point going to bed again. He was dirty and sticky. His feet were so hot and wet that he could feel the inside of his shoes as though he were wearing no socks. Three changes of socks a day would not have been enough to cope with the tropical conditions created by St. Nathaniel's heating system. There was just time for a bath and then some breakfast before the eight-thirty ward round. He felt uneasy that after the events of the past five hours his thinking was dominated by the competing claims of his feet and his stomach. But not washing his feet would be of no help to Henry now.

He had just put one foot into the bath water when his bleeper went off again. He swore and then quickly washed and dried the one foot, put the same socks back on again and answered the bleep. He was summoned to the casualty dapartment, where the new houseman was finding it difficult to cope with someone who had taken an overdose and wanted to discharge herself against medical advice. As Stephen entered casualty he was enveloped by the familiar smell of stale alcohol, vomit and unwashed feet. He was met by one of the staff nurses.

'It's Eileen again. Third time this month. Says she wants to discharge herself but refuses to sign her own discharge.'

Eileen was a regular at St. Nathaniel's – an urban nomad who, when not in police custody, migrated between various hostels, the Embankment, the Barbican complex and the hospital. She was nineteen, fat and spotty – an habitual overdoser with no home, no family, no friends and a personality the psychiatrists termed inadequate. He usual tipple was a handful of valium – or whatever else she could lay her hands on – washed down with a bottle of cider. If she could get hold of a syringe, she would crush the tablets and inject them mixed with water from the tap.

'What have you taken, Eileen?' asked Stephen.

'What do you care?'

Stephen looked down at the latest entry in her three-inch-thick medical file.

'Paracetamol wasn't it?'

'What if it sodding well was?'

'If it was paracetamol, and if you don't sodding well let us do something, you could sodding well die.'

'What do I care if I do die?'

'How many did you take and when?'

'That's for you to sodding well find out.'

'Give us your arm, Eileen.'

'You're not going to stick any of your sodding needles into me.'

But she offered no resistance. The staff nurse reminded Stephen that Eileen was a Hepatitis B carrier. Having put on gloves he drew off some blood and set up an intravenous line. A yellow warning label was stuck to each specimen bottle and each accompanying form. The whole caboodle was then placed into a sealed polythene bag for transport to the chemical pathology laboratory. It would be useless asking a porter to take the specimens even if they had come from a patient who was not a Hepatitis B carrier. In an attempt to amend for not being able to deal with Eileen, Paul Goss – the new houseman – offered to take them to the lab. Stephen and the nurse walked back to Eileen.

'And if you think you're going to wash my sodding stomach out, I'll have you for assault. . .'

But again she did not resist and swallowed with ease the rubber tube pushed between her lips. The staff nurse raised the funnel attached to the tubing and poured in a pint of water. When the water could no longer be seen in the semi-transparent tube, she lowered the funnel below the level of the bed. A foul, acid, yellow-green froth containing fragments of tablets and strings of slime poured out into a stainless steel bowl on the floor. Most patients heaved and retched but not Eileen – it was all so effortless. Stephen turned to leave. Of the two things in medicine that he could not watch, one was eye surgery and the other stomach wash-outs. Once out of casualty his thoughts returned to the question of whether to wash or to eat. The stomach won.

On his way to the canteen he met Gwynneth Morgan, the senior house officer on the Metabolic Unit.

'I heard about poor old Henry Price,' she said. 'Were you there?'

'Yes. I was there, see. I was there,' replied Stephen in an attempt to imitate Gwynneth's accent which owed more to Calcutta than Cardiff.

He instantly regretted his facetiousness so soon after the event. But he need not have worried. Gwynneth was impervious to such incongruities. That was part of what attracted him to her. Her invulnerability and insensitivity combined with her irrepressible energy and unquestioning enthusiasm for her work and career amounted to a kind of innocence. She never looked tired, was always well-scrubbed and knew everything which went on in the hospital as soon as it happened. She had flawless skin and a wide-eyed expression but otherwise hers was a face difficult to remember. The sight of her neat figure in its stiff, clean, white coat breezing along the hospital corridors always stirred in him a destructive kind of desire, an urge to disturb her self-possession and upset her uncomplicated view of the world.

At the self-service canteen Gwynneth opted for a yoghurt and an apple. She usually had the same for lunch as well. Stephen could never understand how some women could function so well on such a diet. After a night on duty he liked to fortify himself with the kind of meal despised by nutritionists but specialised in by hospital canteens – fried bread, two eggs and three rashers of bacon swimming in a tasty salty grease which, when unobserved, he liked to mop up with ready-sliced white bread.

'Why did he do it?' asked Gwynneth as they sat down at their usual table. 'Was he simply tired of being turned down for consultancies? Or was there something else we don't know about?'

'If you don't know, Gwynneth, then I'm sure no one else in the hospital does. Anyway, we don't know that he killed himself.'

'It wouldn't surprise me really if he did. I always thought he was a bit odd.'

Gwynneth's concept of oddness in men was based on whether they chatted her up or flirted with her. If they didn't, they were odd. Stephen thought better of voicing this view.

'If you mean he didn't drink with the boys and he published no fatuous research papers, I suppose he was odd, yes. But I just can't believe he'd kill himself. If becoming a consultant was so important to him, he could always have side-stepped into Rehabilitation or Geriatrics.'

'Who was the first there?' asked Gwynneth.

'I was. And for the first time I actually got there before Resus Reggie.'

'No. I mean who found the body?'

'Sorry. I'm not with you, Gwynneth.'

'I was just wondering who found the body. I mean someone must have rung switchboard and asked for a cardiac arrest call.'

She looked at her watch, stood up, put the apple in her pocket and bustled out of the canteen tossing the empty yoghurt container into the nearest bin with customary accuracy. It was typical of Gwynneth's kind of intelligence to hit the nail directly on the head without seeing the deeper significance of what she had said. She had provided Stephen with a concrete reason for the unease he felt about the whole business of Henry Price's death. Someone must have rung the switchboard asking for the cardiac arrest team, but why in that case was no one there when he arrived. He leant back in his chair, pushed away what was left of his breakfast and determined to contact the switchboard later and find out who made the arrest call. He looked at the clock on the canteen wall. Seeing it was already half past eight, he hurried to Ward 3A.

CHAPTER TWO

As he strode along the speckled marble floor of the corridor leading to Ward 3A, he found himself catching up with the pear-shaped figure of the new houseman, Paul Goss. Paul was only twenty-four but looked more like forty. Even as a first-year student he had looked almost middle-aged. His girth, his thinning black hair and the dark stubble on his chin were complemented by the lace-up black shoes and grey check trousers he wore. His white coat was always buttoned up at the front and he always wore a club tie – either the St. Nathaniel's Golfing or Gilbert and Sullivan Society. He had an expensive-looking gold watch on his left wrist worn with the dial on the same side as the palm; on his fourth finger was a large gold signet ring. Stephen caught up with him just as he was pushing through the swing-doors into the ward. Outside the ward office Sister Mason was busying herself with the trolley containing the medical notes. Her face was even paler than usual. She was obviously upset and fighting back the tears. News travelled fast at St. Nathaniel's. As ward sister she had accompanied Henry Price on hundreds of ward rounds and was bound to miss the quiet, methodical and tactful way he sorted out the medical problems on the ward.

'You've heard?' asked Stephen softly.

'Yes. I can't believe it.'

'Neither can I.'

Stephen walked on into the office. To his amazement Professor Carling was there in person sitting at the desk, sipping a cup of tea and flicking through the nursing register. His fair hair was beginning to grey at the temples but his sun-tanned slightly military looks still seemed too young for the half-moons perched on his nose. It was rare for him to

17

come to the ward even to see the rheumatology patients. But to come and see the flotsam and jetsam admitted under his name as acute medical emergencies was unheard of. Without acknowledging Stephen or looking up from the nursing register, he began to speak.

'I see we have had twelve so-called emergency admissions. If we exclude the four overdoses, the average age of these admissions is well over eighty. Am I to presume they will be blocking my beds for the next six weeks? And will what is supposed to be the Rheumatology Unit become the dumping-ground for the rejects of the geriatric, psychiatric and social services, the deficiencies of which seem to grow in direct proportion to the increasing amount of money diverted their way?'

Although in the interrogative, the question required no reply. Stephen very much doubted if Carling had ever taken the trouble to walk down the road to visit the old workhouse, which served as a geriatric hospital, and see how hard-pressed it was. He seemed unaware of the fact that St. Nathaniel's was supposed to be a district general hospital and open to all-comers and not just the more exotic forms of joint, blood and hormone disorders on which the hospital's fame rested. It was more than Stephen's career was worth to voice these thoughts out loud but he could not let Carling get away with it completely.

'We are usually able to transfer most of them elsewhere after a few days,' he protested feebly.

The professor took no notice, stood up wearily and headed for the ward.

'Right, let's get it over with. Let's see what this great capital city of ours has expectorated in the last twenty-four hours.'

They trouped towards the ward in a diamond formation – the tall figure of Carling at the front, followed by Stephen and Sister Mason and then Paul Goss bringing up the rear with the notes-trolley. Before they reached the main part of the ward, the professor stopped outside the side-room; through its window could be seen a man of about thirty sitting up in bed with a cup of coffee and a newspaper.

'That's not one of my patients, is it?' said Carling turning to Sister Mason. 'And he doesn't look particularly ill to me. What's so special about him that he's managed to get a room of his own on my ward?'

'He's being barrier nursed,' she replied.

'I can see that, but what's supposed to be wrong with him?'

'He's being investigated for AIDS.'

'Ah, of course, that explains everything, doesn't it?' he said with heavy sarcasm. 'AIDS is the fashionable diagnosis in this hospital these days and homosexuals are a favoured group.'

'Actually he's a haemophiliac,' Sister Mason countered, but Carling affected not to have heard her.

The procession continued on to the main part of the ward. Those patients who were able turned their heads expectantly towards the professor. The room was sixty feet long and partially divided in two by a head-high wooden and frosted-glass partition. Beds projected into the room from the walls and from each side of the partition. They started on the left. The first patient was an alcoholic in her sixties who had vomited several bowlfuls of blood the previous evening. Carling stood at the end of the bed and nodded vaguely towards the dull-eyed yellow face propped unnaturally on a mountain of pillows. The blood she had lost was being replaced by a tranfusion into her left arm. It was her third blood transfusion in the last year. On ward rounds it was customary for the houseman to recount a brief history of the patient and a synopsis of the physical findings and investigations. But the shock of Henry Price's absence and Carling's unprecedented presence on a routine business round combined with sheer physical tiredness to strike Paul Goss dumb. While Paul fumbled helplessly through the patient's voluminous medical record, Stephen decided it would be less embarassing all round if he provided the history himself. He loathed – but by necessity had grown proficient at – the end-of-the-bed discussion of patient's details. There were always three or four other patients within earshot. They could hardly be expected not to be listening behind the cover of their newspapers. As a result Stephen employed the maximum of medical jargon. With expressions such as "E.T.O.H." for alcohol and "hepatic necrosis" for cirrhosis of the liver, a minimal kind of confidentiality was preserved but only at the cost of further mystifying and scaring the patient. When Stephen had completed the story, Carling moved away from the bed without addressing a word to the patient.

'Get the liver boys to take this one over.'

He had already taken three steps away from the bed, when Stephen managed to whisper that this deteriorating piece of humanity was the wife of a member of parliament. Carling stood still for a second and turned round slowly in such a way that he almost completely disguised the fact that he had walked away from the patient. He sat down on the side of the bed and laid his hand on hers.

19

'Good morning, Mrs. Rayner. I'm Professor Carling and I am the consultant in charge of last night's admitting medical team. I have discussed your case in some detail with Dr. Hobbs. As you know, the bleeding has come from enlarged veins in your gullet which are the result of your liver problem. Now that the immediate danger is past, we will be handing over to our gastroenterological colleague, Dr. Makepeace, whom I believe you already know. If there's anything you need, please don't hesitate to ask Sister Mason or Dr. Hobbs.'

'When can I go home, doctor?' Mrs. Rayner's dry crusted lips whispered.

'That's for Dr. Makepeace to decide.'

Carling tried to draw away but she had a strong grip on his wrist.

'I'm so sorry. I'm sorry . . .' she said without changing her distant expression.

'That's quite all right. That's what we're here for, Mrs. Rayner.'

With a smile he pulled back her fingers using his free hand and momentarily patted her shoulder. He stood up and the procession moved on. Before he reached the next bed, Carling stopped and turned to Sister Mason.

'I see, sister, that we have a new house physician. Is it the latest fashion among housemen to regard ward rounds as a kind of spectator sport? If it is, I trust Dr. Hobbs will disabuse this new houseman of the notion that spectating will ever find favour on my ward. Regardless of what may be the practice elsewhere in the hospital.'

When they reached the next patient, Paul Goss did his best to make amends. He should not have bothered.

'Mrs. Edna Hewitt is a ninety-two year-old normocephalic caucasian widow and retired schoolteacher in no acute distress who was admitted from home via casualty at six twenty-five p.m. yesterday evening . . .'

Paul was quite right that Mrs. Hewitt was in no acute distress. She was barely rousable and virtually beyond distress. The professor turned once again to Sister Mason.

'And while he's about it, perhaps Dr. Hobbs will advise the houseman that the shape of someone's head and the colour of her skin is apparent from the end of the bed.'

While Paul Goss was beginning to doubt his calling to a career in medicine, Stephen continued the tale of Mrs. Hewitt. She had lived with her daughter completely independently until six months ago. Then at four o'clock one morning she was found at Liverpool Street station partially clothed and trying to catch a train to work. She wandered the next few nights as well. On the fifth night she fell and broke her hip which was pinned at St. Nathaniel's. By the time she was discharged home she had stopped washing, almost stopped eating and more often than not was incontinent. She no longer came downstairs and soon would not even leave her room. For the month before her admission she was bed-ridden. Bedsores followed. She ceased to recognise her family, and at any time of the night or day she might start shouting for no reason. On the day of admission her grandson had been helping her on to the commode; she slipped and the result was a fracture-dislocation of the shoulder. The orthopaedic surgeons said nothing could be done. By then she was stuporous, had developed pneumonia and was in too poor a condition to return home. She had become a "medical case" and was transferred to Ward 3A.

'What antibiotic is she on?' asked Carling.

'We decided not to treat her pneumonia,' replied Stephen.

'And who is "we"?'

'The family. I had a long talk with them and together we decided it would be unkind and inappropriate to give her antibiotics.'

'And as she refuses to take anything by mouth,' said Sister Mason, 'any antibiotics would have to be given as injections.'

'We have all been taking too much for granted simply on account of this patient's age,' rejoined the professor. 'She must be given the benefit of the doubt. Dehydration may be most of the problem. Intravenous fluids and antibiotics might make all the difference. We can't just write her off.'

'But even if she did recover,' continued Sister Mason, 'she will still be demented and incontinent, and she will still have bedsores and a useless painful shoulder. What would you want done, professor, if it was your mother?'

Stephen looked at Sister Mason with an admiration he had never felt before. He could have kissed her for having the courage to say what he was thinking but did not dare utter. He had always respected her professionally but had previously regarded her as rather quiet and ordinary, even mousey. Carling did not answer her question but turned to Paul Goss.

'Make yourself useful and go and fetch some dextrose-saline. Put up a drip and write her up for ampicillin six hourly.'

Stephen groaned inwardly at the thought of Paul Goss's pudgy hands pushing a cannula through Mrs. Hewitt's paper-thin skin into her friable veins. Professor Carling had never shown any interest in the management of the non-rheumatological patients before and had always left everything to his junior medical staff. So why did he have to pick on poor Mrs. Hewitt to demonstrate that he could and would alter his juniors' management for the sole purpose of reminding everyone who was in charge?

In the next bed Eileen, the habitual overdoser, sat propped up like a queen. Stephen had hardly started describing her career of self-destruction when she suddenly spoke.

'Where's Dr. Price?'

'He's not here, Eileen,' replied Stephen.

'Where is he? I want to see him. I'll talk to him but no one else. I won't discharge myself until I see him.'

The thought of Eileen being on Ward 3A indefinitely was too much for the professor.

'We are trying to conduct a ward round, my girl,' he said. 'We have plenty of other patients to see and we can't stand around discussing the whereabouts of Dr. Price. You can't see him and that's that. Would you kindly let us get on?'

She turned to Sister Mason.

'And who's that sodding ponce?'

Before anyone could answer, Carling made his excuses and told Stephen to complete the round without him. Instead of leaving the ward he walked down to the far end of the room. He paused at each of the beds labelled with his name, picking up the treatment charts and making adjustments to them.

'Come on. Tell me what the sod's happened to Dr. Price.'

'I think you better tell her,' said Sister Mason.

Stephen sat on the edge of Eileen's bed and started to half-explain as quietly as he could.

'Eileen, I'm afraid Dr. Price has died . . . It happened last night.'

'I don't believe you. I spoke to him yesterday evening.'

'I'm afraid it's true, Eileen,' said Sister Mason.

Eileen glanced at each of their faces in turn. Suddenly she threw her head back on to the pillows and began to pummel the mattress with her fists. Then she began to scream.

'No! No! No! No! No! No! Who could have done such a thing? He's the only one who ever helped me.'

Sister Mason put her arms round Eileen and managed to quiet her.

'He died suddenly. No one knows why yet?'

After a few seconds Eileen abruptly stopped crying, lay back and stared at the ceiling. When Stephen and Sister Mason reached the next bed, Eileen started to repeat over and over again loud enough for the whole ward to hear.

'Somebody's killed Dr. Price. Somebody's killed Dr. Price but they don't know who. Somebody's killed Dr. Price.'

On the other side of the ward Professor Carling irritably made adjustments to the last few treatment charts and swept out through the swing doors. Sister Mason and Stephen continued on their way as though nothing out of the ordinary was happening and returned to Mrs. Hewitt's bed, where Paul Goss was about to make his second attempt to cannulate a vein. The site of his first attempt was marked by a bruise the size of a 2p piece. Paul looked up apologetically.

'It's easy enough to get in but then the vein just sort of disintegrates.'

'Don't worry, Paul. Veins like that are always difficult. Just write in the notes that she was impossible to set up a drip on,' said Stephen as Sister Mason dismantled the intravenous giving set and called a student nurse to take it away.

'But the professor . . .'

'Quite frankly, Paul, bugger the professor.'

Paul still looked doubtful.

'The chances that he will come back onto the ward are minimal. If the impossible happens and he does, I'll take the can. Let's get on with the round.'

Eventually when they had finished sorting out all the loose ends left over from the night before they retreated to sister's office for tea and biscuits and chocolates left by grateful patients. Sister Mason poured out bisuits and chocolates left by grateful patients. Sister Mason poured out three cups of tea.

'Sister,' began Stephen, 'I'd like to congratulate you on the way you tackled Carling.'

'I don't know why I bothered. It didn't make any difference.'

'Not at all. It was obvious he knew you were right. He was unable to give you a reasonable answer. For the man who is usually never short of an answer that's quite an achievement.'

'But it didn't do Mrs. Hewitt any good.'

'But at least you had the guts to say it which is more than I did.'

'It's easier for me. I will never need a reference from him.'

'Talking of references,' said Paul,' do you think he'll ever give me a reference? Do you think he'll even sign me up after what happened?'

'Oh you've nothing to worry about,' replied Stephen, 'he's probably already forgotten about it. He does that to every new houseman. It's just the reflex exercise of absolute power. You'll get his standard reference at the end of your six months.'

'Are you sure?'

'Of course. The more junior you are the less you have to fear from him.'

'What do you mean?'

'The nearer you are to his level and the more indispensable you are to him, the more poisonous he can be. Did you know Henry Price once applied for an associate professorship in the States?'

'No.'

'Well he did. And you know the reference Carling gave him?'

'No.'

'"As far as I know this man has no criminal record".'

'Why did he do that?'

'Well. Carling may be a lot of things but he's not daft. He realised that Henry was the person who really kept the day-to-day running of the department going.'

'I know,' said Sister Mason, 'that you're not Carling's greatest fan – neither am I – but you can't possibly believe that old story.'

'I know it sounds ridiculous. It's so outrageous that if you put it in a book, no one would believe it. But it's true.'

'How do you know? Who told you?'

'I forget. But whoever told me swore it was true.'

Sister Mason gave one of her rare smiles.

'The fact is, Stephen, you'd like it to be true.'

'You may scoff,' said Stephen smiling, 'but I believe he's capable of almost anything.'

'I've heard that story before. It's just typical St. Nathaniel's Hospital gossip. It wouldn't surprise me if it originated from Carling himself.'

After that no one could think of anything further to say, and the mention of Henry's name cast a gloom over the normally pleasant "tea with sister" interlude – the very time at which Henry would normally have been lighting up one of his sweet-smelling French cigarettes. A student nurse came in with a pile of treatment charts. Sister Mason began to look through them.

'What's Carling been adding to the charts?' asked Stephen with little interest.

'He hasn't added anything. He's been crossing things out. He's stopped everyone's haloprofen.'

'Here let me see,' said Stephen coming over to sister's desk.

He quickly looked through the charts of all the rheumatology patients.

'What's he playing at? He's stopped it on every single patient.'

*　　*　　*

The odd circumstances of Henry Price's death and now the professor's deletion of haloprofen from the drug charts refused to leave Stephen's mind. But he was too weary to make sense of them. What he needed before he could think more clearly was a good hot bath. As soon as he had finished his tea and biscuits he went directly to the second-floor bathroom in the doctors' residence. A minute later he was lying in the bath and letting the tiredness and stickiness ebb away from him. When he had ducked several times under the water to rinse the shampoo from his hair, he began to examine the events of the night and their implications. Who was it who rang the hospital switchboard? Why did Professor Carling just happen to be in the hospital at two in the morning? Although the evidence pointed to suicide, he found it difficult to accept. Surely he would have noticed that something was wrong, if Henry had been intent on killing himself. But then a wave of guilt hit him: guilt that he – and everyone else – might have been too wrapped up in their own concerns to see how depressed Henry had been.

Once dressed, and feeling human again in clean shirt and socks, he made his way to the library to see what he could find out about haloprofen. It was too recent a drug to have anything more than a mention in the standard textbooks of pharmacology. The most he could find was a brief resumé in the "Data Sheet Compendium", a compilation of the product information sheets issued by the drug manufacturers. It told him nothing more than he already knew. Haloprofen was manufactured by Meissner of Zürich. It was another in the long line of anti-inflammatory pain-killers developed in the last twenty years to satisfy the craving of the public and the medical profession for something more novel than aspirin. It was slightly different from its rivals in one respect: it had been shown experimentally to have an effect on the metabolism of rabbit cartilage, which theoretically might prove helpful in delaying the progression of certain forms of arthritis. Stpehen recalled a "New Hope for Arthritis Sufferers" article in the newspapers one year ago. There had also been a television report which featured Professor Carling hinting at a new dawn in anti-rheumatic therapy. Under the heading of "side-effects" were listed peptic ulceration, gastro-intestinal disturbances, fluid retention and rarely blood disorders. Was there some new side-effect that had only recently become apparent? Or had one of the recognised side-effects been occurring much more frequently and fiercely than anticipated?

He was just closing the book when his bleeper went off. It was a flustered Paul Goss with the news that Eileen had "discharged herself against medical advice". Stephen told him not to worry. The level of paracetamol in her blood had turned out to be lower than necessitated treatment, and she would probably be back before too long anyway.

After a lunch of fish and chips and apple crumble it was time for the "Follow-up Clinic": four to five hours of chronic rheumatoid arthritis and osteoarthritis. Stephen's job was to record any deterioration in terms of pain, stiffness and function and monitor treatment for possible side-effects. Although he found it hard to sustain his interest for the whole afternoon, he never failed to be impressed by the way some patients with apalling deformities accepted with equanimity the steady disintegration of their joints and their increasing dependence on others. He often fantasised about what he would do in the same predicament – unable to get out of a chair, unable to hold a pen properly or undo buttons with the splayed out swan-necked digits that projected uselessly from the knuckles. He doubted that he would ever bear such disabilities with such patience.

At every Friday afternoon clinic there were ten new patients. Henry Price used to see them and call Stephen in to show him anything of especial interest. But today Henry's death meant that Professor Carling would have to be there to see all the new cases – something he had not done for at least six months. Before the clinic began, he beckoned Stephen over to the receptionist's desk where he was leafing through some medical notes.

'I want you to stop haloprofen in all patients taking it.'

Before Stephen had a chance to ask why, Carling had disappeared into his consulting room. Stephen picked up the top set of notes and looked across at the patients sitting patiently in rows. He could never understand the rationale behind the organisation of the Rheumatology Clinic. To start with the third floor of the out-patient building seemed a strange place to expect near-invalids to get to. When the lifts failed, it was chaos. A second anomaly was that the patients were not given individual appointment times but told to turn up at one-thirty, two o'clock, two-thirty and so on. This resulted in some patients having to wait considerable time before being seen. Those who relied on hospital transport for getting home again sometimes spent three or four hours at the hospital in order to receive the benefit of ten minutes with a doctor. But some of them enjoyed the clinic as an afternoon out with the only expense being the cost of a cup of tea and fruit-cake from the W.V.S. canteen. Stephen called the first follow-up patient in.

As the afternoon wore on Stephen discontinued haloprofen in several patients. This was easier than he anticipated. He met little protest and very few questions. A couple of patients were clearly relieved. Another was brave enough to confess that he didn't really think it was helping. It was as though they had only taken the drug to please the doctor rather than themselves. It made Stephen uncomfortable to reflect that these unquestioning and passive people were just the kind that doctors and nurses referred to as "good patients". Mrs. English, however, was different. She found haloprofen marvellous and resisted any idea of stopping it. Stephen crossed the corridor to seek the professor's advice. Carling expressed no surprise but some irritation at the phenomenon of a patient with a will of her own. He strode across to Stephen's consulting room and closed the door behind him. Stephen could not quite make out what was being said. Carling was using his authoritative but reasonable voice – a voice which made contradiction impossible. Two minutes later he emerged, walked past Stephen saying 'Give her naproxen instead' and went back into his room.

The patient appeared mollified and entirely adjusted to the idea of life without haloprofen.

'What did the professor say, Mrs. English?' asked Stephen.

'He said in the short term haloprofen worked well and was safe, but in the long term it lost its effect and side-effects might appear.'

'What side-effects?'

'You mean to say you don't know, Dr. Hobbs?' said Mrs. English indignantly.

'Of course I know what the side-effects could be. But did he mention any particular one?'

'No. I didn't ask him.'

It was galling to Stephen that Carling could be more persuasive with two minutes than he could with a quarter of an hour's gentle reasoning.

The professor left at four o'clock leaving Stephen alone in the clinic. By five-thirty the last patient had gone and it was time to dictate letters to the patients' G.P.s. It had just gone six o'clock when he came to the last letter. He placed a new tape in the dictating machine and yawned.

'Letter to Dr. Challenor . . . re. Mrs. Muriel English . . . Dear Dr. Challenor, I reviewed your patient in the clinic today. Her clinical condition remains unchanged. Her haemoglobin is still slightly low at 10.4. Her lymphocyte count is also a little low at 0.8 but this is of doubtful significance. We will repeat it on her next visit in two months' time. Professor Carling has stopped her haloprofen and started her on naproxen 500mg. twice daily instead . . . Yours sincerely, et cetera, et cetera . . .'

Stephen switched off the dictating machine with relief at a tedious task completed. But he then realised that Mrs. English had changed her general practitioner and that her blood pressure had been mildly raised. Wearily he rewound the tape back to the beginning and flicked the switch to replay. To his surprise the tape had neither been wiped clean nor completely rewound and he found himself listening to the familiar rather expressionless tones of Henry Price's voice.

'Continued from the previous tape . . . But the virus is such a common finding among sufferers that it is probably of no significance. On the other hand retroviruses such . . .'

There followed a short whistle, a click and then 'Letter to Dr. Challenor . . . re. Mrs. Muriel English . . . '. Stephen rewound the tape and listened again first to the fragment of Henry's voice and then the rest of the tape. He tried the other side and listened to fifteen minutes of unbroken hiss. He listened again to the begining of the tape. There was nothing strange about hearing Henry's voice on a Rheumatology Department tape but Stephen was puzzled by the mention of viruses, which as far as he knew were of little relevance to rheumatology. He imagined that Henry was trying to tell him something from the grave but there was no medium to interpret the message.

When he had re-recorded the letter on Mrs. English and taken the notes and the tapes to the secretary's office, he returned to Ward 3A for a final review of the patients with Paul Goss. Eileen had indeed discharged herself, the M.P.'s wife had been transferred to the care of the liver team and Mrs. Edna Hewitt had died. The chronic bronchitics were happily coughing up mounds of phlegm, the post-coronary patients were under control, the pneumothorax was steadily reinflating his collapsed lung and the shrinks had reduced the number of overdose patients on the ward. There were no loose ends left and a week-end off duty stretched before him. The time had come to initiate Paul Goss into the Friday evening ritual of a pint or two in "The Apple and Pears".

CHAPTER THREE

"The Apple and Pears" was half way down a narrow one-way street and was overshadowed on one side by St. Nathaniel's parish church and on the other by a disused warehouse with boarded up windows. Stephen had arranged to meet Gwynneth there before going to see a film she had not stopped talking about for the past fortnight. It was not the sort of pub he would ordinarily have patronised. It was cramped and expensive, its unrivalled proximity to St. Nathaniel's allowing it to overcharge with impunity. But Friday evening at "The Apple and Pears" was as much of a routine as the Friday morning ward round and Friday afternoon clinic.

As usual Stephen's glasses steamed up as soon as he entered. With difficulty he spotted Gwynneth perched high on a bar-stool by the imitation log fire. She looked as though she had been installed there for some time. As the mist began to clear from his lenses, he could see she was listening animatedly to the wit and wisdom of Owen Hesketh-Jones, ex-united hospitals rugby captain and now consultant gastric surgeon and father of six children he hardly ever saw. A cardiology senior registrar with a droopy moustache, whose name he could not remember, was bringing her another campari. Peals of Gwynneth's shrill laughter could be heard across the saloon bar. Clearly she found Hesketh-Jones's bar-room monologue much more interesting and amusing than Stephen had ever done. She caught sight of him and tilted her head to one side in an almost imperceptible acknowledgement. He smiled back mechanically.

'Stephen, are you going out with the lovely Dr. Morgan?' asked Paul Goss with a lubricious smile.

'Not really. I just see her somethimes. We were in the same year as students.'

'What's she like?'

Stephen was not sure what Paul was getting at but he didn't like the direction he thought their conversation might be leading.

'Why do you ask?'

'Well, I just thought . . .'

'She's actually very nice. You shouldn't believe everything you hear. What would you like to drink?'

'Oh thankyou. I'll have a half of diet-lager.'

'I never knew such a thing existed.'

Stephen ordered Paul's drink and a pint of bitter for himself. Before long Paul had edged his way into a group of his contemporaries a few feet further along the bar. Soon he was giving them his version of the events of the night before. Stephen was not sure which he found the more offensive: that people were gossiping about Henry or that others had things more important to chat about. He gulped his bitter and stared across into the lounge bar. It was a minute before he realised he was looking straight at Sister Mason. She was sitting with a couple of friends and had a gin and tonic in front of her. She looked quite different out of uniform – more graceful, more worldly and more humorous. Her hair was down and both longer and blonder than he had imagined. Stephen was compelled to admit that it was sheer prejudice that made him surprised to see her in "The Apple and Pears". It just did not fit in with his previous view of her as a dedicated career nurse. The only thing he had got right about her was that she was not one of the regular St. Nathaniel's crowd. She looked up and gave him a quick but warm smile before turning back to her companions. Stephen thought a moment and then picked up his beer and walked round to the lounge bar. He was just about to ask if he could sit down at her table when Gwynneth's voice stopped him.

'There you are, Stephen. What on earth brought you round here? We better get going. It starts in thirty minutes.'

Not for the first time he felt embarrassed by his association with Gwynneth. He knew that nurses did not like her. One half of him had always assumed that it was due to her undisguised ambition, self-confidence and friendliness with the male medical staff. The other half of him had its doubts about a woman who did not seem to have any close friends of her own sex. But there was more than that which made him feel acutely uncomfortable: it was Sister Mason. For some reason he would far rather that she had never seen him in the company of Gwynneth Morgan. He dimly realised that what he craved was Sister Mason's approval.

It was a short drive to the "Forum" cinema in Islington where "Le Métier des Vaches" was showing. They took their seats among a sea of pale, concerned and self-consciously interesting faces, on which perched every conceivable shape of metal-rimmed spectacles – hexagonal, octagonal, ovoid, rectangular, square and even plain round. If the film had been British or American and in colour, the scenes of casual violence and brutal sex would have ensured its classification as an "exploitation movie". But the director was French and famous. And because the film was shot in black and white at a funereal pace, it had been hailed as a "subtle and multi-textured masterpiece". Stephen managed to survive twenty minutes of multi-textured subtlety before his chin dropped on to his chest and sleep overwhelmed him. He eventually woke when the people in the next seats started to get up. He stood up too but sat down again as soon as he realised that Gwynneth showed no signs of moving. She sat gazing wide-eyed at the screen until the last credit had rolled in much the same way as the pious knelt longer than anyone else at the end of a communion service. At last she did get up. Still dozy and slightly unsteady, Stephen followed her out of the cinema indignant at the waste of his precious Friday evening.

'Marvellous, wasn't it?' breathed Gwynneth.

'A truly significant gesture of the human spirit.'

But sarcasm was wasted on Gwynneth.

'You can't have seen much. You were asleep most of the time,' she said.

'Then why ask me what I thought of it?'

Stephen was spoiling for a fight or at the very least some kind of heated reaction. He had desperately wanted to talk to her about Henry on the way to the cinema, but she was not interested and had changed the subject.

'What films do you really like, Stephen?'

'On Friday nights after a hard night on call I'd settle for a good Clint Eastwood.'

'You can't be serious.'

'I have never been more serious about anything in my life,' he said without the flicker of a smile.

Gwynneth laughed and slipped her arm into his. He stiffened. That was one of the things that had begun to irritate him most about her: the fact that it was impossible to needle her or shake her view of the world.

Ten minutes later they arrived at the Tufnell Park flat she shared with two other Welsh girls: one an accountant and the other a solicitor who worked for the prosecution department at Scotland Yard. Although he had been there several times, he had never actually seen any of her flatmates. She never mentioned them either. Stephen asked if he could use the phone.

'Write your call in there,' said Gwynneth pointing to a book by the phone in which each of the girls recorded every call she made.

He did as he was told and fished out ten pence in two pence pieces from his pocket. He placed them in the glass pig intended for visitors' phone-calls and dialled.

'St. Nathaniel's Hospital. Can I help you?'

'This is Dr. Hobbs here . . . of the Rheumatology Department . . .'

'Yes dear? . . .'

It was difficult to tell whether she was the same switchboard operator as last night. They all seemed to speak with the same low-pitched slightly suggestive voice, which gave the impression that they knew every little corner of every doctor's private life.

'Would you mind me asking whether you were working last night?'

'No.'

'You mean you weren't working?'

'No. I mean I don't mind you asking.'

'You mean you were on the switchboard last night?'

'Yes. But I'm free for the next two nights if you're free.'

'No. I . . .'

'Shame . . . You just wanted to hear my voice, did you? Or perhaps do a spot of heavy breathing?'

'No. I just wanted to ask whether you took the cardiac arrest call for the doctors' residence last night.'

'For Dr. Price you mean?'

'Yes.'

'As a matter of fact I did, yes. By the way the name's Maureen.'

'Can you remember who it was who called the switchboard?'

'I might if you call me Maureen.'

'Can you remember, Maureen?'

'No . . . not really . . .'

'Was it a man or a woman?'

'A man. Why are you so interested?'

'Because nobody seems to know who it was.'

'The voice was rather faint and difficult to hear properly. It sounded a little like . . .'

'Yes? . . .'

'I know it sounds a bit silly but in this job you get to recognise certain voices . . .'

'Go on . . .'

'Well . . . when I first took the call, I thought it sounded rather like Dr. Price himself . . . but it couldn't have been, could it?'

'What made you think it sounded like him? Surely you can't always be sure who's ringing the switchboard?'

'No. But I had already spoken to him twice before that night. He had a couple of outside calls.'

'Did he sound depressed at all or upset when you spoke to him the other times?'

'No. I don't think so.'

'And can you remember which extension the arrest call came from?'

'It was from the doctors' residence.'

'Which room?'

'It's impossible to tell with this telephone system u...ess it comes from one of the bedrooms . . .'

'So if it didn't come from one of the bedrooms, it must have been from one of the extensions at the top of each flight of stairs.'

'I wouldn't know, love. I've never been in the doctors' residence, let alone up the stairs. Perhaps you'd like to show me one day?'

'Maureen, I don't know how to thank you. You're wonderful.'

'Recognition at last. And now I must love you and leave you. I've got two more calls coming in. It was nice while it lasted.'

The line went dead. Stephen bounced into the cluttered sitting-room.

'It was Henry. It was Henry himself.'

'What are you talking about, Stephen?' asked Gwynneth.

'It was Henry who made his own arrest call.'

'How do you know?'

'The switchboard operator just told me.'

'Impossible.'

She handed him some toasted cheese and glass of yesterday's chianti.

'But don't you see? If Henry had really been suicidal, he would hardly have rung the switchboard for the resuscitation team, would he?'

'Obviously it was not Henry. Just someone who sounded a little like him. Did the switchboard operator say she was absolutely sure it was him?'

'No but . . .'

'Well, there you are then. I don't understand why you can't take things at face value. He locked himself into the cubicle and then injected himself with a huge dose of insulin. Do we really need a reason when he was found with two empty vials of insulin and a used syringe in his hand?'

'I know it looks like that but . . .'

'Face the facts, Stephen. Henry Price was a no-hoper. Professionally he had nowhere to go.'

'Only because of the stupid way the medical hierarchy works.'

'And as you've always said about him, no one knew anything about his private life or any problems he might have had outside the hospital. The people who make a proper job of killing themselves are never the ones who go about advertising their misery.'

A wave of depression swept over Stephen. He finished the glass of wine and followed Gwynneth into the kitchen where she was washing the plates. He looked around for a tea-towel and did the drying up.

'I suppose you're right,' he said.

'Of course I'm right.'

She turned to him, took the tea-towel from him and put her arms around his neck.

'Give yourself a break, Stephen. Stop acting as though you were in some way personally responsible for what happened. Come to bed.'

She kissed him. He responded half-heartedly. She led him into the bedroom. The divan bed was neatly made and on top of the pillow lay a teddy bear at least three feet tall. She removed it and sat it on the dressing table. She undid the buttons of her blouse to reveal a black bra, walked over to Stephen and removed his glasses. She looked round for somewhere to put them and placed them on her teddy bear's nose. They were a perfect fit. Then she kissed Stephen in such a firm and prolonged way that he felt it would be extremely rude if he were the first to break the kiss. Dutifully his tongue delved as is expected on these occasions. At last Gwynneth drew away and in a quick movement removed her blouse. It crackled with static. Stephen wondered whether she had any clothes that were not of man-made fibre. He sat on the side of the bed and began to remove his tie. She undressed quickly and slipped into bed. Almost as soon as he was alongside her, she aroused and straddled him reaching an efficient climax. He was left with the empty feeling that with increasing predictability had followed their recent love-making. Gwynneth turned over and went to the bathroom. On her return she put on a blue polyester nightie, got into bed and started to read the most recent "Lancet". After a few minutes Stephen got up.

'Sorry. I must get home,' he said.

'Okay. That's fine by me,' she replied.

On his way home to Stoke Newington Stephen reflected that he would not be spending the night with Gwynneth again. He was more relieved than sorry, even mildly elated. The more time he spent with her, the more her way of drawing him into her view of the world – and medicine in particular – grated. He was thankful their relationship was not a talking-point at St. Nathaniels, and its demise would pass unnoticed. Neither of them would have to endure their affair being autopsied by inquisitive friends. He was grateful it had all petered out with so little unpleasantness.

*   *   *

Stephen slept very little that night. He was unable to get out of his mind the image of Henry Price's lifeless body curled up on the lavatory floor and his white coat hanging neatly on the hook. The other image that would not go away was the contrast between his ginger hair and the greyness of his face. Most of the dead people Stephen had seen were old and their thinning white or grey hair seemed in keeping with the waxy pallor of death. But Henry's reddish thatch looked incongruous, not ready for death despite the silvering of the sideburns. At about five in the morning he woke from a light doze with an uncomfortable thought. If Henry had given himself a large injection of insulin, shouldn't they have given more fifty per cent dextrose than they did? Might he then have survived? But Reg Dicks knew what he was doing and would have suggested more if it had been indicated.

Stephen rotated through almost every point of the compass in the attempt to get back to sleep. He had promised himself a lie-in to make up the backlog of sleep his body needed. But body and mind would not co-operate. Even lying in his favourite position on his right side made no difference. At seven-thirty he admitted defeat, got up and had a bath to the accompaniment of the Saturday morning radio programmes on farmers' and religious affairs. After toast and marmalade he sat down with a cup of coffee and a copy of "Recent Advances in Medicine", in which he began to read about the genetics of diabetes. He would soon be taking the final part of the examination for membership of the Royal College of Physicians and he needed to squeeze in a lot of reading before then. But he could not concentrate. His eyes became heavy and kept closing and jumbled thoughts about Henry and his family kept recurring: he must write to send his condolences or perhaps it would be better still to call. He read the same page twice and registered nothing. He put on a cassette of a Mozart piano concerto to try and keep awake. His drowsiness was abruptly ended when his hand relaxed allowing hot coffee to pour on to the book and into his lap. He leapt up and hurried out of his trousers and underpants. That was often the trouble after a hard night on call; when you wanted to sleep, you couldn't and when you wanted to keep awake, you fell asleep. He abandoned any idea of revising for the membership exam. Somehow he would have to keep himself awake for the rest of the day. Then he might have a chance of getting a good sleep that night. It would be difficult to stay awake if he stayed alone in the flat, and ringing Gwynneth was out of the question. The rugby international on the television should take care of the afternoon and he was going to dinner that evening with Justin Rugwood and his wife. There remained the problem of the morning.

He found Henry's home address in the Rheumatology Department office at the hospital. To his surprise it was near Primose Hill. He had never associated Henry with affluence or suspected he might have such an up-market address. A Citroen Deux Chevaux or the nostalgic chic of an old Morris Minor might have fitted in, but Stephen's P-registration purple Austin Allegro was definitely out of place as it strained round the corner into Chiltern Crescent N.W.1. He parked his car and found number 17. It was a large solid Edwardian house with imposing steps leading up to the heavy front door. In the car-port at the side was a white Audi sports car with a St. Nathaniel's sticker on its windscreen. There was no sign of Henry's blue mini. Stephen imagined it standing forgotten in the hospital car park. He surveyed the house and found his gaze returned by a face at a third-storey window. The face disappeared and he climbed the steps. Instead of a front doorbell there was a small metal box with a grille and a red button. Above was a notice: "Press the button and speak your name into the grille". Wishing he had stayed at home he obeyed the instructions.

'This is Stephen Hobbs from St. Nathaniel's.'

It was too late to run away. But what on earth did he think he was doing here? What was he going to say? It was not even as though he was a close friend.

The door opened with a buzzing sound and he stepped into the hall. The door had opened electronically and no one was there to greet him. To the left of the door was a wheelchair and at the foot of the stairs a chair-lift. In an alcove in the wall two priapic African wood-carvings lurked under the leaves of a rubber plant. Stephen looked up. At the top of the stairs a man in a fawn corduroy suit was standing. He had short fair hair and straight well-proportioned features. It was the same man who had stood at the window. He was vaguely familiar but Stephen could not place him.

'Yes?' was the man's sole greeting.

'I'm sorry,' started Stephen, 'I pressed the bell and the door opened.'

'Yes. Angela must have let you in.'

'I'm Stephen Hobbs. I worked with Henry Price at St. Nathaniel's. I was his S.H.O. on the Rheumatology Unit.'

No reply came.

'I decided I ought to . . . would like to . . . tell Mrs. Price how sorry I am and how much I valued working with Henry.'

'That's extremely thoughtful of you. I know she would be very touched that someone from St. Nathaniel's had taken the trouble to call. Not surprisingly she is not too well at the moment.'

'Yes, of course. I'm sorry. It's a bad time to come . . . I'll go. Perhaps you could just tell her I called.'

Stephen turned to leave, welcoming an excuse not to confront her.

'No. Don't go. I'll see if she would like to see you. Come in and take a seat.'

He was taken into a large well-furnished sitting-room with french windows that led to a balcony and overlooked a frost-covered rambling unkempt garden below.

'What did you say your name was?'

'Stephen Hobbs.'

'Make yourself at home. I'll be back in a moment.'

The walls of the sitting-room were lined with books – mainly novels and anthropological and travel books on Africa. One bookshelf stood out as rather different and was lined with children's books. Stephen took a closer look and saw they were mostly written by Angela Price. Half of them were about the adventures of two small boys called "Much" and "Many" and had titles like "Much and Many go to sea", "Much and Many meet the Queen" and "Much and Many go to Africa". Another shelf contained several monographs on immunology and the virology of tropical diseases. On the grand piano in the corner were some family photographs. One picture was of two red-haired boys in school uniforms aged about ten and twelve. Another was of a girl of about twenty. She had long straight fair hair with laughing eyes that had a little too much mascara on them and the kind of sleeveless blouse that had been fashionable in the early sixties. In two silver frames were the overposed studio portraits of a prosperous-looking middle-aged couple who Stephen guessed must be Angela Price's parents. On the far end of the piano was a black and white picture of a man in army corporal's uniform and his new bride – a family likeness suggested they were Henry's parents. It looked as though the money came from Angela's family.

The man in the corduroy suit came back into the room.

'Yes. She would like to see you. Come upstairs.'

They climbed the stairs and entered a spacious bedroom. Jutting out from the far wall was a double bed. A nurse was tidying the bedclothes. When she moved away, Stephen's attention was drawn to an emaciated and motionless body which scarcely ruffled the overlying duvet. An expressionless ageless face lay slightly propped up but quite still on two pillows. Only the eyes showed any life. They were the only feature that reminded Stephen of the lively sixties girl whose photograph sat on the grand piano downstairs. Within reach of the mouth was an object resembling the stem of a smoker's pipe, which was connected by flexible ringed metal tubing to a complicated piece of apparatus by the side of the bed. The most prominent feature of the machinery was a screen two foot by two foot and divided into squares each containing a letter or a number. Her chin rested on a small support like the chin-rest of a violin. On the table next to the screen were a typewriter, a telephone, a television set and a radio. Stephen recognised the apparatus as a

"Possum": a system which by sucking on the tube could type, telephone turn on the television and radio and open the front door. Angela Price was in the late stages of a severe progressive neurological disease. Her arms and legs were useless. Before long she would become unable to cough or swallow her own saliva and finally unable to breathe. A cold might be enough to end her life.

Stephen stood awkwardly just inside the doorway.

'Go and sit on the edge of the bed,' said the man in the corduroy suit. 'Otherwise you won't be able to hear her.'

Stephen sat on the bed. There was no expression in the lower half of the face but her eyes were brimming with tears.

'It's very nice of you to come,' she said in a whisper. 'Henry spoke of you. He liked you. Spoke of you as a kindred spirit.'

Stephen was surprised and flattered.

'I just wanted to tell you how sorry I am and how much I enjoyed working with him.'

His words seemed trite and totally inadequate.

'He enjoyed working with you. He said you had a healthy lack of ambition.'

More like a lack of purpose, thought Stephen. A series of tears rolled down both cheeks. She tried unsuccessfully to catch them with her tongue.

'There should be some tissues on the table. Could you wipe my face, please?'

He mopped away her tears.

'Thankyou,' she said.

There followed an unbearable silence Stephen felt compelled to break. But his words sounded fatuous as soon as they left his lips.

'If there's anything I can do, please let me know . . .'

What could anyone do? How cruel and pointless it all seemed.

'That's very kind of you. I'll remember what you said. But I have a nurse around the clock and Richard has been wonderful helping me sort out Henry's things. Poor Henry. I never realised how unhappy he must have been. Why didn't he tell me?'

More tears streamed down her face and Stephen was almost relieved that it gave him something positive to do. He felt his own eyes begin to prick.

'But we won't know for sure what actually happened until the post mortem has been done. Things may not be as they appear,' he said.

'But looking back I knew something was wrong. He had been unwell and I could see he had lost weight. Every morning he had diarrhoea. But he kept saying he would be all right and recently he had been a little better.'

He looked across at Richard whose unusually pale blue eyes told him it was time to leave.

'Perhaps I better go now. I just . . . Let me say again how very sorry I am.'

'Thankyou for coming. Please come again.'

As Richard showed him out, Stephen noticed a small gold stud in his left ear. He longed to ask Richard who he was and how he fitted in with the Price family, but the latter's polite coolness would have been a deterrent even if he had been able to think of an acceptable way of quizzing him. The cold air in the street was a relief to him. He looked back at the house to see if he was being watched. But he could see no face at any of the windows. Chiding himself for his suspicious instincts he got into his car and drove home.

CHAPTER FOUR

'You're becoming obsessed, Stephen,' said Justin Rugwood.

'Something's not quite right. I know it.'

'Like what?'

'For a start I'm sure Carling knows something.'

'Admit it. You have no hard facts . . .'

'Except for the fact that he was in the hospital when Henry died . . .' interrupted Stephen.

'Coincidence.'

'It would have to be one hell of a coincidence. How often do you think he's in the hospital at two in the morning?'

'Probably just getting his leg over with one of the night sisters or something.'

'It wouldn't surprise me if he was doing that as well.'

'As well as what?' asked Justin.

'Oh, I don't know.'

'You'd really like to implicate him in Henry's death, wouldn't you?'

'He's such a flaming shit. To think I was impressed by him as a student.'

It was Tuesday evening and both of them were on call. They were having a cup of coffee in the doctors' room in the haematology department where Justin had just finished cross-matching some blood. Stephen was on duty again for acute medical admissions. Justin was a senior house officer in pathology. Part of his duties was to be on the night and weekend rota for haematology and blood transfusion. They had been friends since their first day at medical school when they met over a cadaver in the Anatomy Department. As well as dissecting the same corpse they had done their biochemistry practicals together and later practised taking blood from each other. During their last two years as students they shared the basement flat in Stoke Newington that Stephen still lived in. Unlike his friend, Justin had known as soon as he had entered medical school that he was going to be an immunologist and had suffered no setbacks on the way. He always sailed through exams without the slightest difficulty and gained distinctions in two subjects in his finals. Having passed the membership examination of the Royal College of Physicians at the earliest possible opportunity, he had switched to a post which rotated through the various pathology specialities as preparation for becoming an immunologist. But by no means had he been a swot as a student. He had managed to be one of the lads without sinking into the direst extremes of medical student depravity. He got drunk and was rowdy with the best of them, but always drew back from the theft of policemen's helmets and street signs, from throwing up in restaurants and peeing into Rolls Royces' petrol tanks. In contrast to Stephen's congenitally tousled appearance and air of perpetual harassment, Justin's looks and manner were ideal for a young doctor. He was neither too tall nor too short, neither too fat nor too thin. His well-shaped head and face were capped by well-cut dark brown hair. He was personable and quietly confident without any hint of flashiness or conceitedness, and everything he did was done with great precision and economy of action.

'Got any more papers coming out?' asked Stephen.

'Nothing much. Just a case report and an audit review of the department computer.'

'I don't know how you can be bothered, Justin.'

'To borrow and distort the words of the Duke of Wellington, it's a case of publish *or* be damned. Otherwise you'll end up with the Henry Price Syndrome.'

'I thought you had something big lined up.'

'What made you think that?'

'You remember. You told me about it three months ago.'

'Oh that. It all fell through.'

'What was it? You never did tell me.'

'Oh it was nothing much. Couldn't get the funds. Actually, and I know you're going to groan, the computer is a lot more interesting than you would think. It's an amazing machine. Come and have a look.'

They walked out of the Haematology Department and went upstairs to the Immunology Department. Stephen could not help feeling rather pleased that his friend's big project had fallen through. Since qualification their friendship had acquired a slight edge. To Stephen's mind Justin had changed. Once finals were over Justin had moved into a completely new gear. He recognised that in order to get on it was not enough to be bright and reasonably conscientious. You couldn't just wait for the right appointments to fall into your lap; you had to go out and make them come your way. To Stephen it appeared that everything Justin did was a calculated step on the way to becoming a consultant immunologist at a teaching hospital. He read the journals thoroughly as soon as they came out and grabbed every opportunity to get his name in print. He attended all the right meetings and asked pertinent – never impertinent – questions. To Justin's mind Stephen's problem was that he had *not* changed. His disillusionment with the whole medical enterprise was the product of a certain pride, which expected the world to recognise his abilities and find a niche for him without his ever stooping to any form of self-promotion or kowtowing.

The Immunology Department computer was the brainchild of Iain Hamish, the professor of immunology. Its memory contained the results of every blood test done on every in-patient and out-patient seen at St. Nathaniel's. Justin began to punch its keys.

'For example,' said Justin, 'if for some obscure reason you wanted to know how many cases of pernicious anaemia passed through the hallowed portals of St. Nathaniel's in the past year, you just bang a few keys and there you are . . .'

A list in alphabetical order of pernicious anaemia sufferers was spelt out in luminous green–yellow on the computer's display screen. Stephen did his best to appear unimpressed.

'Terrific. A device for churning out endless data. A substitute for original thought.'

'Come on, Stephen. It won't hurt to admit you are the tiniest bit impressed.'

'Impressed? Of course I am. How could I fail to be? There must be inexhaustible opportunities to churn out the "Retrospective Survey of Iron-defiency in Left-handed Alcoholic Circus Dwarves" type of paper. Does it store the result of every blood test done at the hospital?'

'Oh yes. It certainly does.'

'Punch in Henry Price's name.'

'What for?'

'Apparently he had been unwell for several months before he died.'

'Did he tell you he was ill?' asked Justin surprised.

'No. His wife did.'

'I didn't think he was married.'

'Why not?'

'Just something about him. I can't see him as the family type. When did you see his wife?'

'Last Saturday. She said he had lost weight and had had some diarrhoea.'

'What sort of diarrhoea?'

'That, Justin, is hardly the kind of question you ask a newly bereaved widow. I felt enough of a pillock as it was. Well, come on then!'

'Come on what?'

'Feed Henry's name in?'

'I can't.'

'Why on earth not?'

'The computer's meant to be used for department business only.'

'Don't be so wet, Justin. You were quite happy to show off its abilities a moment ago.'

'The computer's probably not got anything on Henry Price anyway.'

'There's only one way to find out. Feed him in.'

'All right. If it will really make you happy.'

Justin punched some keys. A moment later the words "No Record" appeared on the screen.

'There you are, Stephen. "No Record". Satisfied?'

'Let me have a look,' said Stephen scrutinising the screen. 'Well, no wonder there's "No Record". You've punched in the wrong bloody name, you great berk. You've fed in "Henry Rice".'

Justin tried again. This time Henry Price's name appeared on the visual display followed by his date of birth and the date of his blood specimen. Then came the details of his full bloodcount. Everything was absolutely normal until the read-out reached the white blood cells.

'0.5. That lymphocyte count's a bit on the low side,' said Stephen.

'Reduced lymphocytes don't usually mean very much. They sometimes occur in certain viral infections. The rest of the bloodcount's absolutely plumb normal.'

'Yes, but what interests me is that Henry had his blood tested in the first place. Would he have bothered if he thought he had nothing more than a viral illness? The date of the specimen shows that he must have been ill at least as long ago as the middle of November last year. Can your computer tell who actually took blood from Henry?'

'Usually. Yes. The written results normally include the name of the consultant in charge of the patient's case unless someone has forgotten to put it on the original request form.'

'Can you give me a written print-out?'

Justin pressed two keys and the computer spewed out a written version of Henry Price's bloodcount. No consultant's name was attached to it.

'And what happens to the original form requesting the bloodcount?'

'It's kept for a month and then destroyed.'

'I suppose it's possible that Henry took his own blood and wrote the request form himself.'

'What I don't see, Stephen, is why you can't just accept that Henry killed himself. Surely if he had some serious illness, it would support the existing evidence of suicide?'

'I'm not saying he didn't kill himself. It's just that I think there must be more to it than his failure to get a consultancy. And there's something else that bothers me.'

'What?'

'His wife is dying. She's got some progressive neurological disease.'

'So?'

'She doesn't look as though she's got very long to go. If Henry had been intent on suicide, I would have expected him to wait until after her death.'

'But, Stephen, you could equally well argue the opposite. Perhaps her illness was the final straw and he simply could not cope with it.'

'I can't imagine Henry reacting like that. It doesn't fit in with what I know of his character.'

'Which – let's face it – isn't very much. Hardly anyone seems to have known him well.'

'Then there's still the matter of who rang the switchboard.'

'Did the police ask you whether you knew who it was?'

'No. I suppose they either already knew or assumed it was me.'

'Did you get a chance to express your doubts to the police?'

'I was still stunned at the time and the doubts I now have were scarcely

forming themselves. All they did was take a short statement. I think they'd
already made up their mind it was suicide. And then Carling came along
and whisked the policeman away.'

Justin's bleeper went off and he picked up the nearest phone.

'I'm afraid I've got some more cross-matching to do.'

They left the Immunology Department together.

'And what are you going to do now, Stephen?'

'Take a look at Henry's on-call room.'

'What do you expect to find there?'

'I don't really know. But knowing the cleaners it's quite possible that no
one has been there since last Thursday night.'

Justin smiled and shook his head slowly.

'You're daft, Stephen. Absolutely daft.'

*   *   *

Stephen was right. The cleaners had not been near the room since the
previous Thursday. When he opened the door, he was met by a musty,
gamey and somewhat spicy smell. By the light of the naked light bulb
hanging from the ceiling he located the source of the stink. On the mean
formica-topped table by the window lay the remains of a half-finished
take-away Indian meal. Henry always had a curry at midnight on the
nights he was on duty. Next to the congealed food lay a copy of last
Thursday's "Guardian" open at the Arts page. Could a take-away curry
and the Arts page of the "Guardian" possibly constitute Henry's last wish
on earth? It looked as though his meal had been interrupted. Stephen
picked up the phone by the bed and dialled. As he waited he noticed a
bottle of haloprofen on one corner of the table.

'Switchboard.'

'Is that Maureen?'

'She *is* popular tonight. I'll transfer you.'

'A couple of minutes later Maureen came on to the line. Her tone was
rather different than on the previous Friday night.

'Yes?'

'Is that Maureen?'

'Who wants her?'

'It's Stephen Hobbs here.'

There was no reply.

'Dr. Hobbs of the Rheumatology Department. You know . . . I spoke to you last Friday night . . . about Dr. Price's arrest call . . .'

She remained silent.

'Maureen? Are you there?'

'Yes, I'm here.'

'Good. There's something else I wanted to ask you,' continued Stephen. 'You remember saying that Dr. Price had two calls from outside the hospital in the two hours or so before he died? Can you tell me who they were from?'

'Look, there's nothing more I can tell you.'

'Has someone been telling you not to talk to anyone about that night?'

'Of course not. Why should they?'

'Then why won't you talk to me?'

'It's the supervisor. I've been given a warning . . . told me not to be so chatty and spend so long in conversations that have nothing to do with the work of the hospital. Someone made a complaint. It wasn't you, was it?'

'No. Of course it wasn't me. Please tell me that one thing and I promise I won't ask you any more questions.'

'Well, the first call was from his wife. She was always ringing up. The second was from some man. I didn't know his voice.'

'Was there anything unusual about his voice?'

'You said no more questions.'

'Please, Maureen, it's very important. Tell me anything you can think of. Anything at all.'

'He sounded in a hurry. Impatient.'

'Angry?'

'I suppose he might have been. Yes.'

'At what time was that call?'

'Round about one o'clock.'

'Thankyou very much, Maureen. No more questions I promise.'

Maureen rang off before Stephen had finished his thankyou. He returned his attention to the room. It really was a dismal little place: a perfect illustration of Hobbs's Law of Hospital Accommodation – the quality of the rooms in the doctors' residence varies in inverse proportion to the fame of the hospital in question. His room when he was a house surgeon at Bracknell General Hospital was the best junior doctor's accommodation he had ever experienced. The walls of Henry Price's on-call room were duck-egg green gloss to the height of four feet and above a dingy cream. There was a wash-basin whose constantly dripping tap had etched a brown trail on the enamel. Paint was peeling off the lower half of the radiator in brittle curling flakes; the upper half was disintegrating into rust. In one corner was a divan bed that dipped in the middle like a hammock. Stephen pondered what to do with the half-eaten Indian meal. He couldn't just leave it rotting on the table. Using the tips of his fingers he carefully piled up the foil take-away cartons on top of each other, wrapped them up in the copy of the "Guardian" and took them over to the waste-paper bin. There was not enough room for the stinking package so he removed the contents first. Among these was a month-old copy of the magazine "Time Out". It was open at one of the classified advertisement pages. His eyes were drawn to one of the advertisements which had been circled in red. It was in the lonely hearts section:

"OPEN-MINDED PROFESSIONAL GUY (33) seeks similar for entertainment, travel, possible on-going friendship. Serious only. Tel. 784-6318."

Before he had time to mull this over, his stream of thought was abruptly interrupted by the sound of his cardiac arrest bleeper summoning him at once to the Casualty Department.

*   *   *

'Good of you to spare the time, doctor.'

Reg Dicks was, of course, already there directing operations. There was nothing for Stephen to do. Reg had got a medical student to manage the airway and squeeze the rubber bag connected to it, while he prepared to administer a D.C. shock to the grey torso lying on the resuscitation trolley. He stood like a high priest holding aloft the two electrodes of the defibrillator and waited for the nurse to finish applying the electrode jelly to the patient's chest. His gaunt face was dominated by the wide staring eyes which shone out almost unnaturally from their sharply contoured sockets. He was in his element going through the routine he knew so well and took full advantage of the opportunities for showmanship afforded by the presence of several medical students.

'Start at fifty joules.'

The nurse turned the defibrillator dial to fifty.

'Everyone step well back from the patient – unless you want to experience the shock of your life.'

He applied the electrodes and the chest gave a single convulsive jerk. The trace on the cardiac monitor remained a chaotic up and down scrawl.

'A hundred joules.'

Again there was no change on the trace.

'Put her up to one hundred and fifty.'

This time the jerk of the chest was followed by the restoration of a respectable trace on the monitor. The man's colour improved and the nurses began to prepare for the transfer to the Coronary Care Unit. Instead of packing up his equipment Resus Reggie took the students under his wing and started an impromptu tutorial on resuscitation techniques. His enthusiasm for his subject was obvious. He talked almost melodramatically of the importance of timing and speed, the importance of being thoroughly familiar with the workings of the various items of equipment used in resuscitation. He advised them to take the opportunity – whenever a patient died – to practise inserting an endotracheal tube. To the students he was helpful, patient and encouraging, particularly to the male students with whom he established a boy-scout kind of keenness and camaraderie. The women he addressed as 'love'. His sarcasm and spleen seemed to be kept in reserve for other doctors. It was difficult to be sure exactly how old Reg was but he looked rather old still to be a registrar, which added a certain irony to his comments about Henry Price. The apparent youth of his straight fair hair contrasted oddly with the slightly leathery and wrinkled skin. He should have been a consultant or at least a senior registrar; promotion was usually fairly swift in anaesthetics. Stephen noticed for the first time how thin, and frail, he was. He looked ill, but in spite of it had the strength and energy of a featherweight boxer.

'What else has come in?' Stephen asked Paul Goss who was writing down some blood results that had just been phoned through.

'Just the usual sort of crumble.'

Paul was learning fast. Not only had he now put up twelve drips and done his first lumbar puncture, but he was also spontaneously using junior doctor slang: "crumble" for the most derilict geriatric patients, "G.O.K." for the diagnosis of "God Only Knows", "F.L.K." for "Funny Looking Kid" and "L.M.F." for "Low Moral Fibre". The slang and enigmatic initials were part of the junior doctors' ésprit de corps. They were passwords which signalled membership of a club; their implicit callousness and dismissiveness – hidden from the public to which they referred – afforded a guilty pleasure. But it was a pleasure which soon palled and was usually abandoned within a few years of qualifying.

'Oh yes, I nearly forgot,' added Paul, 'You were right.'

'About what?'

'Eileen.'

'What about her?'

'You said she'd be back and you'll never guess what she took this time.'

'What?'

'Haloprofen.'

'Where the hell did she get hold of it?'

'She nicked it from Ward 3A the last time she was in. Doesn't seem to have done her much harm – just a few coffee-ground vomits.'

'Did she take anything else?'

'I don't think so but I checked her blood for paracetamol and aspirin just in case.'

Paul handed over the piece of paper on which he had written Eileen's blood results.

'Well, they look all right,' said Stephen handing the paper back. 'But what was the point of doing a full bloodcount? You know we're supposed to keep tests on hepatitis B carriers to a minimum. It's hardly likely to show anything and the state spends enough subsidising Eileen's gradual suicide as it is.'

'But you know what the professor's like. If I didn't do a full bloodcount, it would be bound to be the one thing he asked for on the ward round. Anyway it's not completely normal. Look at the lymphocyte count.'

Paul passed the results back to Stephen with an air of righteousness vindicated. The lymphocyte count was 0.3 – well below the normal range of 1.5 to 3. Stephen thought first of Henry Price and then of Mrs. English in last Friday's clinic.

'Right. Where is Eileen? Let's go and see her.'

'She's already discharged herself.'

'Shit! How long ago?'

'About half an hour. Said she was going to search for Dr. Price's killer.'

Stephen stuffed Eileen's results into his pocket and strode purposefully out of the Casualty Department towards the Pathology building.

*　　*　　*

It was not often that Justin was visibly flustered and Stephen was surprised by his tetchiness when he arrived back at the Haematology laboratory.

'You'll have to wait a few minutes, Stephen. There's a panic on in theatre. Ruptured aortic aneurysm. They want another six units. Typical of the bloody cardio-thoracic surgeons: they use up all our stores of blood and the patient dies anyway.'

Such cynicism was unusual for Justin too. While he continued cross-matching blood, he was subjected to an excited Stephen beginning to pour out his recent discoveries.

'For God's sake, Stephen. Just keep quiet for a moment while I finish this off. Go and make some coffee or something.'

Stephen did as he was told. Every now and then he went back to the bloodbank to see how Justin was doing. Ten minutes later when he saw him put the six bags of blood into the fridge ready for collection, he approached Justin again with two cups of coffee.

'Have you calmed down now?'

'Sorry, Stephen. It's those cardio-thoracic surgeons. They expect to get their blood the moment they've asked for it. They seem to think blood is just waiting to be poured out from barrels like beer.'

'Are you ready to hear my story?'

'What story?'

'What I've found out. About Henry Price.'

'Have I any choice?'

'No.'

Stephen told him about the unfinished curry, the two telephone calls Henry had received shortly before his death, the reluctance of Maureen the switchboard operator to talk to him, Eileen's and Mrs. English's low lymphocyte count and how Professor Carling had recently taken all his patients of haloprofen.

'So you think there's some kind of conspiracy in which possible side-effects of haloprofen and Henry Price's death are connected?'

'You must admit there do seem to be a few too many coincidences. It's possible that Henry had been taking haloprofen and . . .'

'But why *should* he have been taking it?'

'God knows. But there was a bottle of the stuff on the table in his room. Presumably he was taking it for the symptoms of the illness he had before he died. Or perhaps it was actually the cause of his illness.'

'Are you trying to say that Henry's death could have been engineered to look like suicide to prevent a scandal? Is that it? Things like that don't happen in real life. Not even Carling would be capable of a stunt like that.'

'But a drug company might.'

'It's an international conspiracy now, is it? You and I, Stephen, live in very different worlds.'

'It's not absolutely impossible.'

'You can't possibly be serious. You have absolutely no evidence that Henry had been taking haloprofen.'

'Apart from his lymphocyte count.'

'But you don't even know that lymphopenia *is* a side-effect of haloprofen.'

'There's one way to find out.'

'How?'

'Can your computer give a list of all patients with lymphopenia in the last three months?'

'That's easy.'

They went upstairs again to the Immunology Department. Justin walked over to the computer and punched the relevant keys. Thirty-four names appeared on the screen, several of which Stephen recognised.

'Could I have a printed copy of each bloodcount, Justin?'

'All right. But no more. I have to write down and account for each copy I withdraw.'

'Just write "for research purposes".'

'One by one the bloodcounts were spat out by the computer. When the last one had come through, Stephen stacked them together and began to look at each one in turn. When he had finished, he sorted them into two piles one of which he thrust triumphantly at Justin.

'And what do you make of that?'

'What do I make of what?'

'Look at that pile I've given you. There's sixteen patients there and if you look for the consultant's name at the foot of each result, you'll see all sixteen are Professor Carling's patients.'

Justin checked through the bloodcounts and, saying nothing, handed them back. Stephen stuffed them into his white coat pocket after first removing the copy of "Time Out". It was still open at the classified advertisement page.

'What's this?' asked Justin picking up the magazine.

'I found it in the waste-paper bin in Henry's on-call room.'

Justin read out aloud the lonely hearts advertisement circled in red.

'Could be difficult to explain if that fell out of your pocket at the wrong moment,' he said.

'Justin.'

'Yes?'

'Do you think Henry could have been . . .'

'No. Of course not.'

'How do you know?'

'I don't. But look at the date. It's over four weeks old. Other people use the senior registrar on-call room.'

'Yes. I'm sure you're right. I didn't really think he was.'

Justin handed the magazine back to Stephen.

'What are you going to do now?'

'Find out whether these patients were all on haloprofen.'

'And then what?'

'Come to tomorrow's "Grand Round" and you'll find out.'

'Stephen, I've got a nasty feeling you're going to do something very stupid.'

'I know what I'm doing.'

'Can't I persuade you to leave sleeping dogs lie?'

'Unlike you, Justin, I don't have a glittering career ahead of me. So I've got nothing to lose. No future to ruin.'

'What exactly are you up to?'

'You'll find out tomorrow. Just a little bit of fishing.'

'With yourself as bait?'

'If you like.'

'You're mad. Whatever it is you're going to do has all the trademarks of something that's bound to blow up in your face.'

'We'll see. But you should be glad, Justin. There'll be something in it for you.'

'And what's that?'

'I'll list you as co-author of my first epoch-shattering publication – "Haloprofen-associated Lymphopenia".'

'Thanks all the same but I'm quite happy to leave you to get all the glory.'

'Justin, what's wrong with you?' asked Stephen smiling. 'I'd never thought I'd live to see the day you turned down the chance to get your name on a paper.'

CHAPTER FIVE

The "Grand Round" was held in the main lecture theatre every Wednesday at noon. Today it was the turn of the Rheumatology Department to present a case of especial interest. Usually a manifestation of a rare condition or a rare presentation or complication of a more common condition was described. Sometimes an association was proposed between a particular disease and certain characteristics of the patient, his diet, his life-style, heredity or the presence of other disease. The presentation of the case was the task of the senior house officer. It was followed by a discussion in which the consultant in charge of the case defended the diagnosis and management. In practice the "Grand Round" was a game in which the consultants attempted to discomfit each other.

Stephen had orginally intended with the professor's approval to present "A Case of Migratory Polyarthritis in Non-lupus Systemic Lupus". The events of the past few days had compelled him to change his subject matter. It had taken him until four o'clock in the morning to find and analyse the notes of those sixteen patients with a low lymphocyte count. His perseverance was rewarded. They had all been taking halo-profen. Fortunately it had been a quiet night with only four admissions none of which posed any problems. This gave him time to spend the rest of the night and morning preparing his presentation. Armed with acrylic pens of three different colours he summarised the important details on transparent sheets, which could be projected on to the screen in the lecture theatre. He finished the last sheet at half-past ten which gave him just enough time for a late breakfast and a quick review of the emergency admissions with Paul Goss. At a quarter to twelve he made his way to the main lecture theatre.

While he aligned and focused the overhead projector and checked and rechecked his transparent sheets were in order, the lecture theatre began to fill up. First to arrive were the medical students. There were solitary earnest ones with pale complexions, their white coat buttons all done up and carrying brief cases heavy with textbooks and jumbo-sized writing pads; pairs or trios of girls, hair tied back and ready to take down every word; larger groups of "rugger-buggers" who sat with their feet resting on the backs of the seats in front, white coats wide open, hands in trouser pockets, their loosely knotted ties revealing undone top shirt buttons. Whatever their appearance the students all made their way to the highest seats at the back of the raked auditorium. The next seats lower down began to fill up with junior medical staff, the housemen and registrars. Below them came a smattering of senior nursing staff followed by a larger group of senior registrars. It was possible to tell the status of almost every member of the audience by the row they sat in. Gwynneth Morgan was one of the few who did not know her place; she was chatting loudly in the fourth row with the cardiology senior registrar with the droopy moustache whose name Stephen could never remember. The only other person breaking rank was Reg Dicks. He sat alone at one end of the second row, making his presence felt by coughing repeatedly. Finally the consultants trickled in to take their places in the first three rows.

The opening skirmish of the "Grand Round" was the contest to make the last and most impressive entrance into the lecture theatre. The finest exponents were generally acknowledged to be Professor Carling and Professor Hamish, the professor of immunology. Occasionally they both had to concede defeat to Dr. Shirley Hayden (Nephrology) or Professor Robert Warschauer (Clinical Pharmacology). But this Wednesday the first round went to the professor of immunology. He timed his entrance perfectly. Not only had Carling been seated in the front row for at least thirty seconds, but Stephen had already put his first transparent sheet on the overhead projector and uttered the words "Today's presentation . . .", when Hamish pushed his way through the swing-doors at the front of the lecture theatre. For extra effect he brought with him a retinue of registrars and researchers which included Justin Rugwood. As always he looked in the mood for combat. Professor Hamish never sat with the other consultants at the front, but always found a place two-thirds of the way back in the auditorium as if to declare himself a man of the people. From this position he would lob his verbal grenades towards the front three rows, from where the opposition could only counter-attack by turning round uncomfortably in their seats and directing their ripostes upwards and backwards. The other way Hamish distanced himself from his consultant peers was by maximising the unprepossessing nature of his appearance. His hair was thin, greasy, colourless and too long – the kind of hair no amount of shampoo would ever improve. His incessant and ostentatious smoking, when walking round the hospital, appeared to afford him a perverse kind of pleasure akin to blaspheming in a cathedral. His white coat was crumpled and stained, his trousers shiny and shapeless above brown hush puppies; instead of a shirt and tie he wore a green polo-neck pullover. The sloppiness of his appearance was offset by the energetic eyes that challenged the world over his gold-rimmed half-moons and the precise Scottish tones with which he deflated his opponents. His whole person proclaimed that he had not become professor by having been at the right school or in the right team, by becoming a freemason or by marrying the boss's daughter.

While Professor Hamish made his way to his customary vantage point, Stephen struggled to suppress instincts to abandon his night's work and return to the safe ground of "non-lupus lupus". But he had no choice. He had left the material for his original presentation in his on-call room. Trying to avoid looking at Carling he began.

'I apologise for today's presentation not being as advertised. Instead of "A Case of Migratory Polyarthritis in Non-lupus Systemic Lupus", I will be presenting a number of cases of lymphopenia associated with the anti-inflammatory agent, haloprofen. I will begin by summarising the first three cases which drew attention to a possible association and then I will give the results of a computer search for other cases of lymphopenia at St. Nathaniel's in the recent past . . .'

Stephen glanced over to where Carling was sitting but was unable to discern any change in his posture or expression. The first transparent sheet projected the essential details of Eileen's latest escapade on to the screen at the front of the lecture theatre.

'The first case is a nineteen year-old woman well-known to the Casualty Department and medical wards of St. Nathaniel's. She's an habitual overdoser who has had over twenty admissions, all of which have been the result of self-poisoning. On her last admission haloprofen tablets were identified in the gastric contents obtained at stomach wash-out. It is not known how many tablets she took on this occasion but three empty bottles of haloprofen were found on her when she arrived at the casualty department. The tablets had not been prescribed but appear to have been stolen from the ward during her last admission five days previously. Together the three bottles could have contained up to ninety tablets. It is also not known whether she took all the tablets in the few hours before coming to the hospital or whether she had taken them during the previous five days as well. The patient discharged herself before further details could be obtained. As can been seen her full bloodcount was normal apart from a lymphopenia of 0.3. The last time a bloodcount was done – five months previously – her lymphocytes were absolutely normal.'

Stephen replaced Eileen's details with those of Mrs. Muriel English.

'The second case is a woman of fifty-eight who has had rheumatoid arthritis of moderate severity for nine years. She had been taking the maximum dose of haloprofen – four hundred milligrams twice a day – for six months. The main joints involved were the knees and the metacarpophalangeal joints of the hand. This particular patient reported subjective improvement and was in fact reluctant to discontinue the drug. Her most recent bloodcount shows a lymphopenia of 0.9. Her last lymphocyte count one month ago was normal. As far as is known she has suffered no ill-effects as a result . . .'

Stephen felt sure that the tremor with which he placed the third transparent sheet on to the pojector must have been visible to at least the front ten rows. This was his trump card. With the exception of Justin, only someone who knew the true explanation of Henry's death would recognise the third case as Henry Price himself. Stephen nearly baulked and went straight on to the computer findings. But, he reasoned, there was nothing to lose. If he were totally mistaken in his suspicions, his fantasy need never be exposed.

'The third case – Mr. H.P. aged forty-one – had been taking haloprofen for three months for aching joints of uncertain cause . . . Whether he benefited clinically is not known because he has moved away from the district and been lost to follow-up. But there is evidence of general malaise, weight loss and the development of persistent diarrhoea. His lymphocyte count was 0.5.

Stephen looked across at Carling as casually as he could. He was still sitting in exactly the same position as before, leaning back in his seat, his arms folded and his head inclined slightly to one side. His handsome but unfriendly features betrayed no anxiety, no anger and not even any surprise. If there were any emotion to be detected, it was one of bored indifference. Stephen felt a wave of disappointment come over him. But what did he expect? It was hardly likely that the professor would start blinking uncontrollably or roll on the floor foaming at the mouth. His sense of righteous indignation having almost deserted him, Stephen pressed on hurriedly.

'Having come across these three lymphopenic patients, all of whom had been taking haloprofen, I made a search for other cases of lymphopenia using the Immunology Department computer. The next transparent sheet gives the total number of St. Nathaniel's patients with a lymphocyte count below 1.0 in the last three months. As you will see, there was a total of thirty-four cases. On reviewing the notes fifteen were – as one would expect – immunosuppressed patients with leukaemia, organ transplants, or on cytotoxic treatment for cancer. In three of the cases no obvious cause could be detected from the notes. The remaining sixteen patients were taking haloprofen for rheumatoid or other forms of arthritis. Although these figures refer only to a fairly small sample of patients, and have not been subjected to detailed statistical analysis, it seems reasonable to conclude that the use of haloprofen is associated with an increased incidence of lymphopenia. Obviously there are many more questions that need answering. For example, what proportion of the total number of people taking haloprofen develop lymphopenia? Is the lymphopenia reversible on stopping the drug and is it of significance in increasing vulnerability to infection or tumour formation? Should haloprofen be withdrawn as an anti-inflammatory agent? And, finally, what are the mechanisms involved in reducing the lymphocyte population?'

The floor was now open for consultants to score points off each other and younger doctors to impress with perceptive comments. Usually there was a pause of half a minute before anyone spoke. But as soon as Stephen finished, Carling took the floor.

'Haloprofen is one of the newest anti-inflammatory drugs on the market and only started its first clinical trials two years ago. It is not in widespread use in the United Kingdom. In fact the Rheumatology Department in this hospital is one of only three centres in the country which have been using the drug on a limited trial basis. The apparent association with lymphopenia has led to haloprofen being discontinued at St. Nathaniel's. This was a necessary but disappointing decision – disappointing because of its beneficial effects in certain patients and because of its unique properties of modifying the metabolism of joint cartilage. Although unexpected, the development of lymphopenia raises the possibility that haloprofen might have had promise in conditions where suppression of the immune system is desirable. But this possibility will now almost certainly never be explored. A report has of course been sent to the Committee of Safety of Medicines.'

Stephen regarded the professor's words as proof that low lymphocyte levels were the reason behind stopping haloprofen in all his patients. That Carling chose not to explain this action could only be construed as an intention to conceal the truth. Whether the inclusion of "Mr. H.P. aged forty-one" had scored a bull's-eye was more difficult to tell. Certainly the relative feebleness of Carling's comments made it clear that Stephen's presentation had discomfited him. By his standards he had done little more than maintain an unruffled front and had placed himself at the mercy of the other consultants.

Professor Hamish had obviously decided to bide his time and let the picadors have first run of the arena. The pause following Carling's brief speech was finally interrupted by the clipped South African accent of Professor Warschauer, a neat diminutive man with a large head and Einstein-like hair and moustache.

'David Carling mentioned that haloprofen was only being used on a "limited trial basis". I would very much like to know how limited this trial basis was. Was the "limited" use of the drug restricted to those sixteen patients with lymphopenia? If not, what proportion were they of the total number?'

'At St. Nathaniel's we have used haloprofen in about one hundred patients altogether,' replied Carling.

'Ah, I see,' Warschauer continued, 'it was being used on what might more accurately be described as an *extended* "limited trial basis" which has revealed an incidence of sixteen per cent for lymphopenia. It seems more than a little surprising that it has taken two years for an incidence of that magnitude to be recognised.'

'*We* have, in fact, only been using the drug for six months. The previous studies revealed only a very few cases of blood disorders with an incidence no greater than with the other anti-inflammatory agents.'

61

Dr. Shirley Hayden decided to take her turn. She was a large woman in her early sixties. She was one of the handful of St. Nathaniel's consultants with an international reputation, which was achieved by a large collection of kidney biopsies performed in the 'fifties under conditions that would not be considered "ethical" in the 'eighties. She was also famous for her tweed suits and calling her housemen "boy".

'I sympathise with the Department of Rheumatology. It is always a disappointment to have to discontinue a drug because of an unexpected side-effect. However, it is some consolation that in the field of anti-inflammatories there are about twenty other similar, safer and cheaper drugs available. So perhaps our grief at the departure of haloprofen from the scene need only be short-lived.'

Various other people made contributions to the discussion. Among them the cardiology senior registrar, whose name Stephen could never remember, made some tedious speculations on possible mechanisms underlying haloprofen's deleterious effects on lymphocytes. This gave him an opportunity to cite his own research on drug-mediated damage to heart muscle. Stephen could not help noticing the appreciative expression on Gwynneth's face as the aspiring cardiologist told the world about his tissue cultures. His irritation served only momentarily to distract him from the question of Professor Hamish's reticence. Why had he said nothing? Especially when Stephen had supplied him with a perfect opportunity to savage Carling. But at last – when Gwynneth's senior registrar had finally run out of things to say – Professor Hamish took the floor.

'Dr. Hobbs is to be congratulated on adding a small footnote to the history of therapeutics. We are indebted to the Department of Rheumatology for bringing to the attention of the world an anti-inflammatory drug with a difference: one that might have had more potential as an immuno-suppressant. But this we will never know. The inevitable attention of the media would make further research on this drug impossible. But perhaps the most important lesson to be learnt from this morning's presentation is the value of computers in monitoring the effects of new drugs . . .'

'I would like to underline Iain Hamish's point about computers,' interrupted Professor Carling. 'Without the Department of Immunology's data bank it might have taken much longer and possibly several deaths before the dangers of haloprofen had been revealed.

Fortunately – although we still need to analyse the inital findings further – the drug has been stopped before any serious consequences have occurred. We can only hope that the powers that be continue to earmark funds for the maintenance of computer systems for clinical and not just administrative purposes.'

'Finally,' continued Hamish, 'I would like to commend the Rheumatology Department for its honesty in presenting a failure of contemporary medicine – so much more instructive than the obscure clever-dick diagnoses which are the usual fare at the Grand Round.'

A short silence followed. The atmosphere was a mixture of surprise and anti-climax. Why had Hamish let Carling off so lightly? What lay behind this unprecedented chumminess between the two men? Once it became clear that no one else had anything to say, the medical students at the back of the lecture theatre began to shuffle in their seats and click their briefcases shut. Grabbing what little of the action was left, Dr. Hayden and Professor Warschauer simultaneously chose to be the first to stand up and leave. The rest of the audience soon followed.

As the auditorium emptied, Justin Rugwood came up to Stephen.

'I knew you had a screw loose, Stephen, but not a death wish. Don't you realise Carling can crucify you? He can see you never work again.'

'I've stopped caring about things like that.'

'What do you care about then?'

'The reason Hamish didn't put the boot in.'

'He didn't have to. You did it for him. Anyway he did quite well out of it. Vindicated his computer.'

Justin rejoined Professor Hamish's retinue. Stephen switched off the overhead projector and gathered together the transparent sheets of his presentation. The sheets spilled out of his hand and he bent down to pick them up again. When he got up, he found Reg Dicks facing him. Reg shook his head and said, 'I suppose you think that's rather clever, don't you?'

Before Stephen had time to ask what he meant, Resus Reggie had moved on. There were now only two people left in the auditorium. Still sitting in the front row was Professor Carling. Ten rows back sat Sister Mason. Carling noticed Stephen's eyes moving from him to the seats further back and turned round to see where he was looking. Sister Mason stood up and left by a door at the back of the lecture theatre. Stephen could scarcely believe what happened next. Carling approached smiling broadly and placed his hand on his shoulder.

'Well done, Stephen. Come to my office at two o'clock and we'll discuss what mileage we can get out of it.'

*   *   *

The only offices in the hospital of any size or comfort were in the administrative building. The clinical departments were all cramped and characterised by clutter. Boxes of laboratory supplies, equipment and journals were stored in every available space – outside lifts, in corridors, in broom cupboards and sometimes even on stairs. The Rheumatology Department was in the basement of a grey three-storey building with small windows and a pointed triangular roof like an inverted "V". To reach it visitors had to descend some dark stone stairs, which were usually the only means of access since the lift seldom worked. Stephen pushed through the heavy portholed swing-doors into the bright strip-lighting of the department's research laboratory, where Keith, Brian, Francesca and Doug were working at a crowded bench trying hard not to dig their elbows into each other. This quartet were the professor's research technicians. Carling treated them well. They were allowed to have frequent coffee breaks, cans of lager at lunch, days off when they had colds and they even got to call the boss David. One of the professor's undeniable gifts was the ability to make them feel part of a vitally important scientific enterprise as they minced, pickled, radioisotoped and microscoped rabbit joint cartilage. In exchange they were paid a pittance. None of them looked up as Stephen walked to the other end of the lab where the professor and his secretary had their offices.

'Can I help you?' asked the secretary momentarily raising her eyes from her knitting. She was a plump woman of about fifty with dyed auburn hair. She was knitting a lilac cardigan identical to the one she was wearing.

'I'm Stephen Hobbs.'

'Yes? . . .'

'Professor Carling's S.H.O.'

'Oh yes, of course. I thought you looked familiar. You young doctors do change so quickly. It's hard to keep track.'

'Is he in?'

'He's expecting you?'

'Yes. At two.'

'You're early. I don't expect he'll mind. Just knock.'

Stephen was just about to knock when he thought of something. He turned again to the secretary.

'There's something I wanted to ask you.'

'Yes?'

'Did you type Dr. Price's letters?'

'His clinic letters. Yes.'

'Did he ever give you anything else to type.'

'Like what?'

'Do you remember ever typing anything for him on the subject of viruses?'

'No. Why do you ask?'

'Well, when I was dictating the letters from last Friday's clinic, one of the tapes I was using had a few seconds of Henry Price saying something about viruses.'

'No. He never gave me anything like that. Perhaps he got his wife to do it.'

'His wife?'

'Yes. She types. Or used to before she got so ill. I'll ask the professor if he knows anything about it.'

'No, I wouldn't do that, thankyou. It's nothing important. I was just curious, that's all.'

'It's no trouble. Honestly.'

'That's very kind of you. But I probably made a mistake. It probably wasn't Dr. Price at all.'

Stephen knocked on the professor's door and entered. There was nothing grand about Carling's office. It was the size of a prison cell. There was only room to walk sideways between the desk and the bookshelves. Carling looked up from his seat as though surprised to see him.

'You asked me to come and see you at two o'clock,' said Stephen awkwardly.

'Oh yes, of course. That's right. Take a seat, Stephen.'

Carling stood up and offered him the only chair in the room. He then sat on the edge of the desk looking down at his S.H.O.

'You should be able to do something with that material, Stephen. You've been sitting around quite long enough. It's high time you got something published. Perhaps a preliminary case report in the first instance and then with a longer period of follow-up something more substantial.'

'I'm sorry I didn't give you any warning . . .'

'That's all right. I must say I would have preferred it if you'd let me know what you were going to do. But I'm glad enough you found out about the lymphopenia before we had any more cases or any serious morbidity.'

'You mean, professor, that you didn't know about the lymphopenia?'

'Of course not. Why should I?'

'But at the meeting you said that a report had been sent to the Committee of Safety of Medicines.'

'Perhaps you could do that later this afternoon. It shouldn't take too long.'

'And you said the department was monitoring the drug for possible side-effects.'

'Yes. *You* have monitored the drug very effectively.'

'There was no formal monitoring programme then?'

'That had already been done in the European trials.'

'Then why did you take everyone off haloprofen, if it wasn't because of the lymphopenia?'

Carling paused a little before answering.

'If you really want to know, there were two reasons. In the first place – in spite of its theoretical promise – it had become clear that it was no better than anything else on the market and was twice as expensive. And secondly . . .' He paused again and went to the door to his secretary's room which Stephen had deliberately left open. 'Teresa, be a love and get us some coffee please' He then closed the door and resumed sitting on the desk. 'The real reason is that those buggers at Meissner of Zürich have decided not renew their research grant to the department. So I was buggered if we were going to continue using their drug.'

Stephen felt all the excitement and nervous expectancy drain away at the banality of the professor's explanation. Not only had Carling been completely ignorant of the unwanted side-effects of haloprofen, but his sole motive for stopping the drug had been pique. For Stephen there was no longer the prospect of uncovering a conspiracy involving his professor and a major drug company to sustain him. He recalled one of the maxims of his old history master at school: when in doubt, always favour the "cock-up" rather than the "conspiracy" theory of history.

The lack of sleep the previous night took hold of him, and suddenly he felt very tired and dispirited.

'They didn't even give me any warning,' continued Carling. 'They just rang up last week and told me. Just like that. It will mean I'll have to lose at least one and possibly two technicians.'

Stephen wondered whether he was meant to feel sorry for the technicians or for Carling.

'What were their reasons for stopping the money?'

'Just the usual stuff about moving into different areas of research and less money available due to rising costs. But your little discovery could prove very useful. At the very least it will cause them some embarrassment: a nice little report in the B.M.J. and a judicious tip-off to the national press. But there is one thing I am curious about, Stephen.'

'Yes?'

'If you thought I already knew about the lymphopenia, why *didn't* you discuss your case presentation with me first?'

This was the question Stephen had been dreading. He had two choices: to tell the truth or fudge. He tried to fudge.

'I only found out about the low lymphocytes last night.'

'But there was time to tell me about it this morning before the "Grand Round".'

After a few seconds' desperate thought he realised his powers of invention were not up to fudging convincingly.

'I didn't want you to know,' he blurted out.

'Why on earth not?'

'I wanted to see what your reaction would be.'

'What for? As some kind of undergraduate prank?'

'No. Nothing like that.'

'Then why?'

'I know it sounds crazy – and, of course, I now know that it's not true – but I had a theory that Meissner and possibly you were involved in some conspiracy to suppress the truth about haloprofen and that someone had died either as a result of the drug or the conspiracy itself.'

Carling let out a series of rather forced unnatural snorts of laughter. But his eyes were not smiling.

'You really loathe me that much, do you? Well, I know people – other doctors anyway – don't particularly like me. And quite frankly I couldn't give a fuck. In fact I have just about had it up to here with St. Nathaniel's bloody hospital. When I first came here ten years ago, the board of governors welcomed me with open arms. So did the rest of the consultants. They said it was long overdue for St. Nathaniel's to have a proper department of rheumatology. They promised me funds, they promised me buildings, they promised me staff. But they gave me nothing. Everything to do with the department I have had to wheel and deal for, fight for, beg for: the lab, the technicians, even my beds on Ward 3A. It's a miracle that the department has any kind of reputation outside Britain, let alone outside London. What reputation we have is in spite of St. Nathaniel's. And just look where it has got us – a cockroach-infested rabbit-warren in a dark cold basement and an office you couldn't even swing a cat in . . .' Carling finally looked at Stephen and noticed the mixture of embarrassment and astoundment on his face and began to talk in quieter more measured tones. 'The point of what I'm saying is – try and understand the way I appear. It's become a way of keeping the head above water and getting things done in the face of the complacent indifference and the vested interests which permeate the whole hospital. The place is riddled with smugness, obstructiveness and inertia. Politics and graft are what being a professor is all about. If you have any time to get any research done, you're damn lucky.'

Stephen looked down at his tie and stared at the pattern hoping for some inspiration as to what to say next. Carling's frustration and anger hung in the room like a bad smell that wouldn't go away, stifling speech. The silence seemed endless.

'You mentioned someone dying,' Carling resumed. 'I don't remember anything like that in your presentation.'

'Not in so many words. No. It was one of the three cases I described.'

'Which one?'

'The third: "Mr. H.P. aged forty-one".' Carling did not react. 'The one with diarrhoea and weight loss.'

It was by now absolutely clear the Stephen's plan had failed utterly. The professor did not know what he was talking about.

'Tell me more about him,' said Carling.

'You didn't notice anything familiar about him?'

'No.'

'It was Henry Price.'

There was a knock on the door. The professor opened it and Teresa walked in with a tray. They waited tensely as she set the tray down on the desk and painstakingly poured out the coffee offering milk and sugar. At last she smiled and went out closing the door behind her. Neither of them touched their coffee.

'What do you mean "Henry Price"? What's he got to do with it?' asked Carling.

'I discovered that he also had a lymphopenia. It struck me as too much of a coincidence.'

'So you added two and two together and got five? And what did you hope to achieve by including him in the presentation?'

'I thought that if there had been a conspiracy, someone would be forced to reveal themselves.'

'And did they?'

'No.'

'Thank God for that.'

Stephen's mood lifted slightly. Carling's last remark implied that perhaps he did know something about Henry's death which he would rather did not become common knowledge.

'How did you find out that Henry Price had a lymphopenia?'

'I simply fed his name into Professor Hamish's computer.'

'Look, Stephen, I think I better tell you about Henry. His lymphopenia had absolutely nothing to do with haloprofen.'

'What was the cause then?'

'What I'm going to tell you must not go beyond this room.'

'It won't. I promise you.'

'The reason Henry had reduced lymphocytes was that he had AIDS.'

Stephen was stunned.

'I don't believe it.'

'I didn't at first. But he told me himself a short while before he died. I asked him how he could be sure and he told me that an axillary lymph node biopsy proved it.'

'Who else knows? Do the police.'

'No. The police don't know. As far as I'm aware the only other person who knows is Bill Kendrick who took the biopsy just before he went to Australia. Most important of all Henry's wife doesn't know. That's why you must keep this strictly to yourself. The suicide is more than enough for poor Angela to be coping with.'

Stephen was forced to face the fact that the professor's behaviour in relation to Henry's death had been entirely honourable and full of consideration towards the Price family.

'But surely,' said Stephen, 'the pathologist must be told. He's not going to be too keen on placing himself at risk.'

'It's too late. The post mortem has already been done. Anyway the risk of infection is fairly minor even if he were to prick himself.'

'But won't the pathologist be able to tell he had AIDS?'

'We'll just have to keep our fingers crossed that he doesn't. After all he wouldn't have been looking for AIDS, and Henry told me that the axilla was the only place there had been any swollen lymph glands. We'll have to hope he doesn't attach too much significance to an isolated finding of lymphopenia.'

Stephen was shattered that his clumsy sleuthing and ill-founded suspicions could have led to scandal and pain.

'I'm terribly sorry. I nearly ruined everything.'

'No. It was very astute of you. There was more to poor Henry's death than met the eye. Anyway something good's come out of it. At least we've got something to give those ungrateful buggers in Zürich a sleepless night or two.'

CHAPTER SIX

Stephen woke at five the next morning. For thirty minutes he struggled to get back to sleep. He had never attended a Coroner's inquest before and his mind would not stop rehearsing his evidence. If he simply stuck to the facts, the coroner need never suspect the truth about Henry Price. But a careless word or gesture might sink him. What if the questioning appeared to be leading relentlessly towards Henry's dark secret? Should he try and divert the Coroner's line of enquiry? Should he pretend he knew nothing? Should he lie if necessary? In Stephen's imagination a series of progessively disastrous consequences spiralled down towards inevitable ruin: humiliation in court, conviction for perjury, newspaper notoriety, a heavy fine (or possibly even prison), dismissal from St. Nathaniel's, being struck off by the General Medical Council and finally abandoned by family and friends.

He switched on the bedside light, put on his glasses and looked at his watch. Five thirty-five. It was no good trying to get back to sleep. He did not want to leave the warmth of his bed either. He knew how cold the bathroom would be. At last he had to give in to the dictates of a full bladder, the relief of which had gained precedence over all other physical needs. He reached for his dressing gown which was draped over the end of the bed and put it on under the duvet. After a count of three he jumped out of bed, scuttled across the room to the electric wall-socket, switched on the blow-heater and hurried to the bathroom. There through the mist of his own breath he noticed powdery dry ice on the inside of the window. He stood over the lavatory bowl. But as his feet became colder and colder nothing happened. He looked down and noticed a creamy discharge. Then to his horror the jet came. It felt as though a red-hot pipe cleaner followed by splinters of glass were rushing through him. Despite the cold his forehead began to sweat and his glasses steamed over. Not only might he have to perjure himself today, but he would also have to submit himself to the indignities of "The Special Clinic". He climbed back into bed taking "Harrison's Principles of Medicine" with him. He carefully read the sections on non-specific urethritis (NSU) and gonorrhoea and placed his money on the latter. He thought of Gwynneth. She would have to know. How would she react? Much more calmly and rationally than himself Stephen decided. He speculated on how many links there might be in the chain of fornication and whether it included the cardiology senior registrar with the droopy moustache and name he could never remember. He tried his hardest to tell himself that it was an infectious disease like any other and any shame was a form of atavism to a repressive and less rational age. He extrapolated the same argument to Henry Price's inquest. Why shouldn't his AIDS become known to the world? Perhaps such a revelation might prove positively beneficial by focusing attention on the tragic consequences of the disease and arousing public awareness and sympathy. No. It would not wash. He did feel ashamed. He did feel grubby and degraded. Conversely, making the truth about Henry public could only achieve further hurt to the Price family and pollute their grief with shame. The honourable thing would be to lie.

At a quarter to ten he entered the glass and concrete building which housed the Coroner's Court. The ground floor was taken up by the probation service and the first was given over to trade licensing and accident prevention. He found the court on the second floor. A uniformed policeman in his early fifties approached him. In his enormous hands he held a pen and clip-board. One corner of his mouth curved upwards as if in enjoyment of some private joke. His voice was incongruously high-pitched, too polite and over-respectful, none of which did anything to put Stephen at ease.

'Good morning, sir. I'm P.C. French, the Coroner's officer. Would I be right in presuming you have business with the court this morning?'

'Yes, replied Stephen.

'And may I ask your name, sir?'

'Yes, of course . . . I'm sorry . . . I'm Dr. Hobbs.'

'Would that be Dr. Stephen Hobbs of St. Nathaniel's Hospital, sir?' said the policeman referring to his clip-board.

'Yes. That's right.'

'Thankyou, sir. Would you be so kind as to follow me and I'll show you where to sit.'

P.C. French led him into the court. It was a surprisingly small room and contained none of the darkly varnished Victorian furniture and fittings Stephen's imagination had envisaged. There was no obvious witness box and it was hard to see where a jury would be housed on the rare occasions when one would be necessary. More than anything else the room resembled the smallest kind of lecture theatre with the seating arranged in an arc facing the Coroner's desk.

'Your first time, is it, sir?' P.C. French stated rather than asked.

'I'm sorry. I'm not quite sure what you mean.'

'Your first time before the Coroner, sir?'

'Yes,' replied Stephen discouraged that it was so obvious.

'Nothing to worry about, sir. Just keep it straightforward. You've got Dr. Hudson. You'll be all right as long as you answer his questions. No more and no less. There are only three kinds of witnesses that get on his wick: those who won't answer the question, those who don't know their facts and clever dicks.'

'What about people who tell lies?' thought Stephen after P.C. French left him sitting alone in the court. He knew he had done nothing wrong but was unable to prevent the same sense of unease and guilt he experienced every time he passed through customs at the airport. A new fear then begun to assail him. What if the coroner thought not enough had been done to save Henry's life? Stephen forced his mind back to the events of that terrible Friday morning and tried to recall each step in the resuscitation attempt. Was some vital procedure omitted? Would he be revealed as a complete incompetent? Perhaps he should have given more dextrose than the syringeful Reg Dicks gave him. He tried to comfort himself that if any mistake had been made, Dicks – as the senior doctor present – would be held more to blame. Physical discomfort now began to add itself to the mental. His bowels were churning and his bladder was close to bursting. He wished he had relieved himself prophylactically before sitting down in the courtroom. It was three minutes before ten and other people were taking their seats. He had left it too late to rush to the lavatory. He tried to shift his attention to the others taking their seats. It was surprising how few of them there were. He turned round and saw the "Richard", who had been at Angela Price's house last Saturday, sitting in the back row. Instead of his corduroy suit he was wearing dark pin-stripe. At one minute to ten Professor Carling walked through the court door, nodded at Stephen and sat down next to Richard. They exchanged a few whispered words. Carling too was uncharacteristically wearing a dark suit. A few seconds later Reg Dicks appeared and was ushered by P.C. French to a seat in the same row as Stephen. Like everyone else in the room – apart from the handful of bored-looking reporters at the back – he was also decked out in dark pin-stripe. So was the Coroner. Stephen was seized by a new panic: his suit was light brown.

The procedure was less formal than Stephen expected and consisted of the coroner asking each witness in turn a series of questions. The first witness was the young police constable who gave an account of the scene he found the previous Friday morning and said there was nothing to suggest foul play. There was no mention of who made the call to the switchboard requesting the resuscitation team. The next witness was a Dr. Peter Farrell. He was in his early forties and of slight build. Stephen had never seen him before.

'How long, Dr. Farrell,' asked the Coroner, 'had you known Dr. Price?'

'About twenty years, sir,' came the reply.

'How long did you know the deceased in the capacity of general practitioner?'

'For eight years. Ever since his return from Africa. I first met him when we were both medical students'

'Would you say you knew him well?'

'I knew him fairly well at medical school, but I only saw him occasionally after that. In recent years I have seen his wife much more frequently than him.'

'She has been extremely ill, has she not, Dr. Farrell?'

'Yes. For the past three years she has been becoming progressively disabled by amyotrophic lateral sclerosis, which is a particular kind of motor neurone disease.'

'The disease is invariably fatal, is it not?'

'Yes.'

'How far has the disease progressed in Mrs. Price's case?'

'She has no power of movement in either her arms or legs and is completely bed-ridden. She has to rely on others for everything. Recently she has been finding it increasingly difficult to swallow.'

'You would, therefore, describe her as being in the advanced stages of the disease?'

'Yes,' replied Dr. Farrell with a hint of irritation in his voice.

'Was Dr. Price depressed by his wife's condition?'

'It would depress any husband.'

'Please avoid general observations and answer the specific question.'

'All the recent conversations between Dr. Price and myself concentrated on his wife. We never talked about his feelings about her illness.'

'And you had never at any time treated him for depression?'

'No.'

'In your visits to Mrs. Price, Dr. Farrell, did she ever express any concern about her husband's well-being?'

'Yes. She told me he had lost weight recently and had intermittent diarrhoea. But she couldn't persuade him to come and see me. She worried too that he still had not found a consultant post despite his long experience in his speciality. She also thought he was working too hard. He was desperately trying to get some research finished.'

That Henry was engaged in some kind of research took Stephen completely by surprise in view of the former's sardonic comments about medical research in general. The Coroner's next question was equally surprising.

'How long had Dr. Price been a diabetic?'

'Since the age of ten.'

'He needed regular insulin injections, didn't he, Dr. Farrell?'

'Yes, sir. He injected himself twice daily with a mixture of long-acting and short-acting insulins – once before breakfast and once before his evening meal.'

'Was his diabetes well-controlled?'

'As far as I know, yes. He regularly checked his own blood glucose.'

'Thankyou, Dr. Farrell. That will be all.'

It was Stephen's turn next. Much to his relief the questions mainly required the answers 'yes' and 'no' or a simple description of the attempts at resuscitation. He was not asked whether he or someone else had called the resuscitation team. The answer to this question came from a most unexpected quarter: the next witness, Reg Dicks.

'Dr. Dicks, you were the person who called the switchboard at the hospital and requested the resuscitation team, were you not?'

'Yes.'

'Can you tell me how that came about?'

'That night I was the duty anaesthetist for the operating theatres and . . .'

'So on the night in question you were not on call in any capacity as part of the emergency resuscitation team?'

'No.'

'Please carry on.'

'I had just finished anaesthetising for an appendicectomy and was climbing the stairs to the third floor in the doctor's residence, when I found Dr. Price lying on the top step.'

'Did you know at the time that it was Dr. Price?'

'No. I recognised him as a doctor on the staff at St. Nathaniel's but couldn't put a name to the face. He didn't have a name badge on his lapel either.'

'Would you describe his condition when you found him?'

'His face was grey and clammy. He also seemed confused, unable to understand what I said and unable to speak.'

'Anything else, Dr. Dicks?'

'He looked as though he was in great pain but he was unable to indicate where. He had also vomited.'

'At that stage he was definitely conscious?'

'Yes, but only just.'

'What did you do when you found him?'

'I felt his pulse. It was fairly rapid at one hundred per minute but regular and reasonably strong. I placed him prone in the recovery position and rang the switchboard from the phone at the top of the stairs.'

Reg Dick's clipped monotone was not unlike Henry Price's voice but its intonation was far less varied. It was surprising, thought Stephen, that Maureen the telephonist could have confused the two. But the request for the resuscitation would have been quick and to the point consisting of only a few hurried words.

'At that stage,' continued the Coroner, 'what did you think was the most likely cause of Dr. Price's condition?'

'I thought a coronary was the most likely thing.'

'What did you do then?'

'I decided to fetch a resuscitation trolley from the Casualty department.'

'Isn't it rather unusual, Dr. Dicks, to leave a patient in the kind of state he was in? Isn't the doctor's responsibility to stay with the patient once help has been summoned?'

'Normally yes. But I knew I could do more for him if I had the wherewithal for resuscitation and I knew I would find a trolley in the foyer of casualty which is immediately next to the entrance of the doctors' residence. I was sure I could get the necessary equipment to Dr. Price quicker than the duty resuscitation registrar who would have to come from the other side of the hospital where the wards are. It was a decision I had to take immediately and when I left Dr. Price his circulation was perfectly adequate.'

Resus Reggie's eyes seemed more staring than ever. He had begun his evidence relaxed but now his slim body was taut as though preparing itself to spring in self-defence. He managed to control his voice but his eyes were full of anger and contempt.

'If you were faced with the same set of circumstances in the future, Dr. Dicks, would you take the same decision?'

'In the unlikely event of being faced with an identical decision, the answer would be yes.'

'When you returned, you found that Dr. Price was no longer at the top of the stairs?'

'That's correct. He was inside a cubicle in the lavatory and the door appeared to be locked from the inside.'

'You found Dr. Hobbs trying to get the door open?'

'Yes.'

'How do you think Dr. Price's body found its way to the cubicle?'

'I suppose he must have had just enough strength to crawl there.'

'Yes, Dr. Dicks, it was probably the last thing he ever did. Had you stayed with him, would you have prevented him from expending the last of his energy in this way?'

Reg had no choice but to answer, 'Yes, I would have stopped him.'

Reg had been brought down by his infatuation with the hardware of medicine. Stephen almost felt sorry for him.

'Thankyou, Dr. Dicks, that will be all,' concluded the Coroner. The Home Office pathologist, Dr. Lionel Winbolt, rattled through his evidence as though he had a further ten autopsies to do that morning. To Stephen's relief no mention was made of any abnormal lymph glands and the biopsy scar in the armpit appeared to have escaped notice. His relief was further increased by learning that his efforts at cardiac compression had not broken any ribs or squashed the heart muscle to pulp. Various complications of diabetes were stated as being present including marked narrowing of the coronary arteries by atherosclerosis. In one of these arteries Dr. Winbolt had found a clot and it was clear that he regarded this as the cause of death. The Coroner asked him whether there was any evidence of insulin overdose. The great man explained that it would be impossible to determine whether this was the case. Measuring insulin levels after death was problematical and interpretation difficult especially when fifty per cent dextrose had been injected.

The Coroner summed up. He found that there was insufficient evidence to sustain a verdict of suicide by the administration of an excessive dose of insulin. He therefore adjudged that Henry Price had died as a result of coronary thrombosis and that diabetes had predisposed the deceased to such an event at a relatively early age. He briefly moralised on how – despite being a doctor – Henry had been a smoker and how this would have increased his susceptibility. Finally he extended his sympathy to the Price family and left the court.

Stephen felt able to relax at last but as a result became acutely aware again of the pressure in his bladder. He walked as quickly as was seemly out of the courtroom and into the lavatory. Any hopes that his early morning symptoms were a transient one-off phenomenon were dashed as once again splinters of broken glass seared through him. There could be no reprieve. He *had* to attend "The Special Clinic". As he left the washroom he consoled himself that at least he had come through the inquest unscathed. He even smiled inwardly at his earlier premonitions of doom. He was just about to descend the stairs when he felt a hand on his shoulder. It was P.C. French.

'Just a moment, sir, I wonder if you would mind coming with me.'

Fear swept over him again. He should have known he could not escape so lightly.

'There's just one more little matter that needs tidying up, sir.'

He followed the large stooping policeman into a windowless office next to the courtroom. He was invited to sit down. P.C. French sat opposite him and unlocked a drawer in the desk between them. He took out a small cash-box and placed it on top of the desk. He chose another key from his crowded key-ring, unlocked the cash-box and counted out two ten-pound notes and one fiver. He put them in an envelope and put them down in front of a bewildered Stephen.

'It's yours, sir. Your fee for court attendance as a medical witness,' explained the Coroner's Officer. 'Would you mind signing that you have received your fee?'

Stephen signed his name in a register book, picked up the money and put it into his jacket pocket. Despite its small bulk its weight nagged in the pocket as though it were blood-money. He thanked the Coroner's Officer and got up to leave.

'By the way, sir,' said P.C. French as Stephen had reached the door of the office, 'court attendance fees are taxable income. So please don't forget to declare it on you next tax form. They'll always catch up with you in the end.'

*   *   *

'One couldn't have asked for a better verdict, could one, Stephen? And while we're on the subject, I would like to congratulate you on the way you gave your evidence. Thank goodness the whole dreadful business is over.'

Becoming Professor Carling's blue-eyed boy was a strange feeling. Flattery is all the more seductive when it comes from someone who has previously done little more than ignore you. The Professor had been extraordinarily friendly in the clinic that afternoon. Over coffee he had even extended an invitation to crew one weekend on his boat at Hayling Island. Stephen shuddered at the thought. Carling went on to drop a hint that he might be considered for the post of research registrar in the department. Stephen was tempted by the idea of two cushy years with an M.D. at the end of it and no nights or weekends on call. But apart from the horrible prospect of two more years with Carling, he had to admit to himself that he had no real interest in research in general or rheumatology in particular.

After the clinic was over he made his way to the St. Nathaniel's V.D. Clinic (euphemistically termed the "Department of Genito-Urinary Medicine"). It was just after five o'clock. Unless medical students had changed since his day, Stephen calculated that none of them would be keen enough still to be at the clinic at this hour. Then there was the question of whether to wear his white coat or not. If there were anyone at the clinic who might recognise him, a white coat might suggest he was there in a professional capacity. On the other hand the white coat might make him more conspicuous. It was a difficult decision. In the end he went as a civilian.

The clinic was for historical reasons of propriety a short distance away from the main hospital. The story was that the board of governors in the late nineteenth century stipulated that a "Special Clinic" could not be within the hospital walls because its presence would give offence to patients, visitors and the nursing staff. Stephen could not help feeling grateful for the prudery of those worthy far-sighted Victorians and did not feel at all inconvenienced by having to cross three streets and a square in order to reach his destination. As he approached the clinic, he looked up and down the street to make sure no one he knew happened to be in the vicinity. His plan was to walk past the entrance and return two minutes later, if he caught sight of a familiar face. Fortunately such an expedient proved unnecessary and he walked straight into the reception area. A pleasant soft-spoken receptionist asked him to write his name and date of birth on a form. In exchange he received a card with the day's date and the number 53 written on it and was asked to go upstairs to the men's clinic. He sat down in one corner of the waiting-room and immediately unfolded a copy of "The Times" which he had brought with him for protection. He hid behind the paper for several minutes but failed to take in anything he read. Eventually curiosity to observe his fellow patients got the better of him. He lowered the paper as casually as he could only to find his gaze returned by the senior registrar in cardiology whose name he could never remember. 'Gwynneth strikes again,' he thought. He tried looking away in a manner that denied recognition and crossed his legs in what he hoped was a relaxed style bringing his right ankle up to rest on his left thigh. A tightness in his calf and an aching in his right hip rapidly made it obvious that this was an impossible position in which to read a newspaper. After a decent interval, when he could bear it no longer, he slowly returned his foot to the floor. There were fifteen other patients in all. Apart from two couples sitting next to each other, everyone left at least two seats between himself and his neighbour. Copping a dose was a great leveller and the victims were a representative cross-section of the male public with the exception of a disproportionate bias towards homosexuals. After twenty minutes the male nurse called out number 52 and the cardiology senior registrar was ushered into one of the doctors' rooms. Stephen was just speculating whether chronologically he should be number 52 and the cardiologist 53, when he was called and guided into a different room.

The doctor was looking at a file and had his back to the door. Below the hem of his white coat, Stephen noticed a pair of fawn-coloured corduroy trousers. The doctor turned, smiled and shook Stephen by the hand.

'Hi. I'm Richard Maynard. We met at Henry's house.'

Stephen tried not to show his surprise. So Richard was not only a friend of the Prices, but a venereologist as well. Surely he must have known that Henry had AIDS.

'Yes, of course,'replied Stephen. 'And you were at the inquest this morning.'

'Angela asked me to go on her behalf.'

'How did she take the verdict?'

'She seemed surprised at first. I think she had made up her mind that Henry had killed himself. But once it had sunk in that he had had a coronary, she was immensely relieved. I think she had been blaming herself in some way. Anyway tell me what brings you here.'

Stephen was forced to shelve his desire to fish for more information about the venereologist's connection with the Prices. He recounted the history of his affliction. His initial embarrassment was soon allayed by Richard's friendly and non-judgemental style of questioning. He felt much as he did when discussing the merits of different kinds of spectacle frames with an attentive optician. Even the examination and the taking of specimens were relatively painless. Richard confirmed that gonorrhoea was the probable diagnosis and gave him a prescription for some oral antibiotics.

'It really was extremely thoughtful of you to have visited Angela. I know she appreciated it,' said Richard when the consultation had finished.

This statement seemed to imply a curiosity to know why Stephen had taken the trouble to call.

'St. Nathaniel's being the unfriendly and impersonal kind of place it is, I thought if I didn't call, then no one would.'

'You were very nearly right. Professor Carling was the only other person from the hospital who called. No one else even so much as put pen to paper except for one of the ward sisters.'

'Sister Mason?'

'That's right. She said how good Henry had been to work with.'

'Yes. He knew more medicine than all the other senior registrars put together and was much more conscientious too. Typical of the system that he should be the one senior registrar who couldn't get a consultancy. All because he refused to churn out papers.'

Richard smiled at Stephen.

'You sound like that's a bee in your bonnet,' he said.

'Perhaps. That's why I was so surprised at something Dr. Farrell said at the inquest.'

'What was that?'

'He said Angela Price had mentioned some research Henry had been doing. Have you any idea what she could have been referring to?'

'I really don't know. Either Angela or Peter Farrell must have got the wrong end of the stick.'

Much as Stephen would have liked to ask more, it was clear Richard Maynard wanted to get on with his clinic. Stephen thanked him, picked up the prescription and went downstairs to the reception desk where he was given a follow-up appointment for ten days' time. He left the clinic and walked to the chemist at the end of the road in order to get the necessary antibiotics. His sense of shame had begun to reassert itself and he reckoned the chance of being recognised was less in an ordinary chemist than in the hospital pharmacy. He was wrong. The assistant at the counter had just taken his prescription, when another prescription was thrust into her hand on his left. He turned his head slowly and once more found himself exchanging stares with the cardiology senior registrar whose name he could never remember. Stephen could not prevent himself blushing. The cardiologist pursed his lips, put his hands in his coat pocket and nodded slightly.

'You did the case presentation on lymphopenia and that anti-rheumatic drug, didn't you?' he asked.

'That's right.'

'Pretty feeble display by Carling I thought. He gave the impression it was the first he had heard of it.'

'It was.'

'And you're still employed?' he asked with a laugh.

'As far as I know, yes. What I couldn't understand was why Professor Hamish didn't put the boot in?'

'Probably owed Carling some political favour.'

The assistant returned and handed each of them an identical package. She kept her eyes lowered but could not resist a quick glance at the two of them. Stephen fancied that she had decided their simultaneous presence and identical prescription indicated their partnership in sin. A side of Stephen wanted to put her right on the fact there was no direct connection between them. But why, he thought, should he care if a complete stranger thought he was gay?

They stepped out again into the street. Stephen would dearly have liked to part company, but they both started off in the same direction towards the hospital. They had taken too many steps for him to change his path to the opposite direction, and it would look ridiculous if he lagged behind or quickened his pace.

'There's not really much point pretending we don't know how each other have been spending the last hour. I'm Damian Ralston, senior registrar in cardiology.'

Stephen had no option.

'Stephen Hobbs, senior house officer in rheumatology.'

'You'll never guess where I got my dose. From another doctor.'

'Really,' replied Stephen.

'Word of warning, old chap. Stay away from a certain Welsh S.H.O. on the Metabolic Unit. God knows where she's been.'

'Really.' It seemed the safest thing to say.

'What about you?'

'Oh, no one you'd know . . . some nurse . . . from another hospital.' He felt ashamed that his lying had more to do with his own protection than chivalry towards Gwynneth.

They walked on in silence. As they approached the hospital, Stephen found to his chagrin that they were still both bound for the same destination, "The Apple and Pears". The cardiologist insisted on making way for Stephen to step inside first. Gwynneth was perched on her stool by the fire listening with rapt attention to the booming tones of Owen Hesketh-Jones. She saw them come in together. If she felt any anxiety, it did not show. The cardiologist, whose name Stephen had already forgotten, offered to buy him a drink.

'What would you like to celebrate with?' he asked.

'I'll have a bitter, please.'

They both sipped their beer. The froth stuck to his companion's droopy moustache. Why on earth, thought Stephen, do people grow such silly moustaches? He could understand beards. But moustaches didn't even have the merit of avoiding shaving. What went through a man's mind when he decided to grow, and when he groomed, his moustache? Every now and then the cardiologist looked over towards Gwynneth. He was obviously more cut up than he let on. He must have seen her as more than a brief affair. Stephen wondered whether he had seen the teddy and the polyester nightie. Eventually the man returned his attention to his drink.

'So you work for Carling. Is he really such a shit?'

'He's hardly ever around. He's always flying off to America, Sweden, Switzerland or God knows where. So I haven't seen enough of him to give an objective opinion of what he's really like.'

'In other words you can't stand him.'

'Something like that, yes. To be fair, though, he hasn't been too bad recently. He's even been turning up in out-patients for the past week.'

'I suppose he's got to since that time-expired senior registrar of his topped himself.'

'The Coroner's verdict was coronary thrombosis.'

'Really? The hospital grapevine has it he was depressed because he couldn't get a consultancy. Exactly how old was he?'

'Forty-one.'

'Christ. That *is* old. I'm thirty-four and I'm already panicking. There's always someone younger, brighter and with more publications at each interview I go to. If I were him, I would certainly have been depressed. And rheumatology too. What possessed him to do rheumatology? All you can do is pat people on the back and give them aspirin . . . or haloprofen.' He laughed loudly at his own joke. 'I think I would have topped myself by now, if I were in rheumatology.'

Stephen winced.

'I gather he had been away in Africa for three years and when he returned no one would give him a job. He was channelled into rheumatology because at that time it was thought to be a rapidly expanding speciality. His other problem was that he had published practically nothing.'

'Then it was his own fault. He must have known the score. If you're too lazy to publish, you get what you deserve.'

'It wasn't laziness. It's just that he spent too much time with patients and had nothing but contempt for career-motivated research of no intellectual or practical merit.'

But the cardiologist had lost interest and was looking over towards Gwynneth again. He turned back briefly.

'But he was doing some kind of research. When I was doing my work on experimental in vitro viral infection of heart muscle, I used to see him occasionally down in the Virology Department.'

'What was he doing there?' Stephen asked eagerly.

But it was too late. The cardiologist's attention had shifted irrevocably. He stood up and drained his second pint.

'Excuse me, old chap. The bitch has got to know. If not for her sake, then for Hesketh-Jones's.'

He crossed the pub to where Owen Hesketh-Jones was holding court. He nodded briefly at the surgeon and turned to Gwynneth. She looked up at Hesketh-Jones, who shrugged his shoulders without interrupting his peroration to the group of junior hospital doctors surrounding him. She grimaced impatiently as the cardiologist took her a short distance away. As he was talking to her, Gwynneth's eyes were directed towards the floor devoid of any expression. After a short while she lifted her head and looked slightly quizzically over towards Stephen. He shook his head and she gave a barely perceptible smile as if to say 'Thanks'. The cardiologist turned round and glared in the direction Gwynneth was looking. But Stephen was ready and had already turned away raising his glass to his lips. The cardiologist left the pub by the other door and Gwynneth returned to her stool. A few minutes later she finished her campari and said goodbye to Hesketh-Jones, putting him out sufficiently to halt his monologue for at least three seconds and pat her on the bottom. She walked over to Stephen. She was just about to speak but he got in first.

'It's all right. I know. You needn't explain anything.'

'Serves us all right really, doesn't it?' she said.

'I suppose it does. I'm thinking of becoming a monk.'

'You wouldn't last a minute.'

'By the way I didn't tell what's-his-name about you and me.'

'Thanks. I couldn't have blamed you if you did. You're a sweet man, Stephen.'

She kissed him lightly on the cheek and looked at him fondly before leaving. Across the room he saw Owen Hesketh-Jones look at him in disbelief. His depression lifted a little and he felt warmed by Gwynneth's gesture. She wasn't such a bad sort after all. He made up his mind to get drunk.

Three pints later Sister Mason and a couple of friends sat down in the other bar. She smiled at him as she stood at the counter collecting three gin and tonics. When she returned to her friends, Stephen moved a yard further along the counter so that he could watch her in the other bar. He studied her minutely, the way she smiled, the way she lifted her glass and flicked her hair back behind her ear. He strained to hear her voice and counted it a bonus when her laugh was loud enough to filter through to his side of the pub. He suddenly wanted her approval more than anything else in the world. He wanted her to wrap him up in her arms and let him bury his face in her neck and cry like a child. Before long he – the great cynic – was fantasizing about walking up the aisle with her. She was a saint. She could be his saviour and rescue him from his rut. But she was on a pedestal. It could never be.

Five pints later Sister Mason and her friends got up and left. Stephen was overwhelmed by depression again. He wallowed in despair even to the extent of buying some cigarettes. He no longer cared who saw him and what anybody thought of him. He lit up and stared vacantly at the miserable saucer of skimpy dry lemon slices "The Apple and Pears" specialised in for gin and tonics. He was just easing himself carefully off the stool in order to navigate his way to the Gents, when a soft voice came from behind him.

'What are you so depressed about? I thought you were Carling's blue-eyed boy these days.'

He turned round unsteadily. It was Sister Mason.

'Can I buy you a drink?' she asked. 'Or have you had enough?'

'No. Let me get you one . . .'

It was too late. She was already ordering. The five pints had coursed through his body and were waiting impatiently to be released.

'Excuse me,' he said, 'I'll be back in a moment.'

He made his way to the Gents. The beer had dulled his senses and diluted the splinters of glass. As he stood over the stinking gully, the little self-esteem he still possessed diminished further. He was not sure there was a God, but he was convinced there was a malign influence at work in the world. The woman he dreamt of had actually come up and spoken to him. And how had she found him? Depressed, drunk and smoking. And when she had offered to buy him a drink, how had he responded? By lurching off for a pee. At least she was ignorant of his morbid affliction. There could be no possible doubt: Someone as nice as Sister Mason could never really like him. Before leaving the Gents, he checked his flies carefully and surveyed his nostrils in the tiny cracked mirror on the wall to check that nothing unwholesome was emerging from them. He rinsed his face and swilled his mouth out several times with the metallic-tasting water. He then noticed there was no towel. The warm air from the electric hand-dryer failed to dry his hands; it proved equally ineffective on his face. He was still bent down with his face under the hand-dryer when Hesketh-Jones entered.

'Dropped some money,' explained Stephen feebly.

He stood up, wiped his face with his handkerchief, his hands on the seat of his trousers and hurried back into the pub.

'Sorry I was so long. I dropped some money.'

'You ought to be more careful, Stephen.'

'You're more right than you'll ever know, Sister Mason.'

'Sally.'

'You're more right than you'll ever know, Sister Sally.'

'Just Sally will do.'

'You haven't got a drink. That won't do. I'll get you one.'

'No thankyou, Stephen. I've got to drive you home.'

'No. I insist. I'll buy you a drink and then I'll drive you home.'

'That's sweet of you but I'm not yet tired of life. I'll drive.'

'You know something? You're probably, almost indubitably, right. Would it offend you terribly if I didn't drink that pint you've just bought me?'

'I think you've made the right decision, Stephen. What you need is some food inside you.'

They walked along to the pizza house at the end of the street. The cold fresh air revived him sufficiently to alert him to the full import of what was happening to him. Yes, it really was true. He was walking down the street with Sister – no, SALLY – Mason and they were about to have a meal together. He resolved to make every effort to improve his act.

The pizzas were nothing special but the meal went well. Conversation flowed easily. They had a good moan about St. Nathaniel's and enjoyed themselves swapping instances of Professor Carling's inflated ego and callousness towards patients and staff. Stephen found Sally a patient audience for his theories about what was wrong with modern medicine: the inappropriate use of technology, the way it distanced patient from doctor and the way clinics for everything from cradle to the grave were undermining people's capacity to look after themselves. In turn Stephen found Sally's discussion of the French Cinema fascinating, particularly her interpretation of 'Le Métier des Vaches', and they arranged to go and see it the following week. Inevitably the conversation turned to Henry Price.

'What happened at the inquest today?' asked Sally.

'The Home Office Pathologist found a clot in one of the coronary arteries and the Coroner gave a verdict of death due to coronary thrombosis.'

'Thank God. I'm glad . . . for his familiy's sake.'

'Did you know Henry was a diabetic?'

'Yes. I did.'

Sally obviously knew more about Henry than Stephen did.

'I never believed it was suicide anyway,' he continued.

'What did you think he died of before the inquest?'

'It seems ridiculous now. I was so stunned and upset by his death that I had a crazy idea he might have been murdered as part of a conspiracy to cover up a scandal about the side effects of haloprofen.'

'So I was right.'

'What do you mean?'

'"H.P. aged forty-one". That was meant to be Henry, wasn't it? That's why I stayed behind at the end of your case presentation. I thought you must have been up to something and I made up my mind to ask you. But with Carling sitting there I thought better of it. What were you trying to achieve?'

Stephen told her about his theory and the conversation with Carling omitting the fact that Henry had AIDS. But Sally was much more interested in Henry than he had anticipated.

'So what was the cause of Henry's low lymphocyte count?' she asked.

Stephen tried to fend her off with talk of a possible viral illness that reduced rather than increased the number of lymphocytes as was usual. She knew he was keeping something back from her.

'There's something you haven't told me. You're a rotten liar and I'm going to keep on badgering you until you tell me.'

'All right, Sally, I'll tell you. But only if you absolutely promise to keep it to yourself.'

'I promise.'

'The reason Henry had a lymphopenia was that he had AIDS.'

Sally looked at Stephen bewildered.

'That's impossible.'

'I couldn't believe it either. But it's true.'

'How do you know?'

'It was confirmed by an axillary lymph node biopsy.'

'How do you know all this?'

'Carling told me.'

'And how did he know?'

'He said Henry told him.'

'But that makes no sense whatsoever. If it were true, Carling would have been the last person in the world Henry would have confided in.'

'That's what I would have thought too,' said Stephen beginning once more to have suspicions about Carling's role in the whole business.

'Anyway I know for a fact it can't be true.'

'Look, how well did any of us really know him?'

'I did.'

Stephen finally realised what she was saying.

'I'm sorry. I had no idea,' said Stephen with a mixture of embarrassment and disappointment.

'Don't worry about it, Stephen. How could you possible have known? It was over a year ago. We didn't exactly advertise the fact.'

'You don't have to tell me about it, if you don't want to.'

But she needed to talk and Stephen was avid to listen. The affair had lasted about three months. It was the only affair she had ever had. They met about once a week and the fact of Angela Price's illness cast an ever-present cloud of guilt over the relationship for both of them. Sally never expected it to last and knew it could never come to anything. But she had been surprised by how abruptly Henry had ended it all. One evening he told her they could not see each other any more except in their day-to-day work. The reason he gave was that his wife only had a short while to live and he owed it to her to spend as much time as possible with her.

'But he was practically always in the hospital.'

'I'm only telling you what he said.'

'Apparently he was involved in some research.'

'Henry? Surely not. I'm sure I would have known about it, if he was.'

'In retrospect,' said Stephen, 'he did change in the last few months. He lost his sense of humour and his unhurried way of doing things. I remember thinking his eyes were different. They had a new kind of urgency, an energy you sometimes see in people who know they're going to die soon.'

'You still believe he had AIDS then?'

'I don't know. I really don't know.'

'Well, I do. I know he wasn't gay,' Sally said with great firmness.

CHAPTER SEVEN

It was Friday evening and just over one week since Henry had died. Stephen decided to visit Angela Price again. He parked his car fifty yards away from 17 Chiltern Crescent. Standing in the car-port was the same white Audi sports car as the last time he visited. He guessed it was Richard Maynard's car and decided to wait a while. Three quarters of an hour later he was still sitting in his car thinking how boring being a private detective must be. He was just about to drive home when Richard emerged from the front door and drove off in the white Audi. He waited two more minutes, got out of the car and pressed the button by the door. He spoke his name into the grille and the door opened.

He climbed the stairs and knocked on the bedroom door. A different nurse from last time opened the door and let him in. He sat down beside the bed. Angela looked even weaker than when he last visited. But the look of alarm had gone from her eyes. Stephen said hello. Feeling less awkward than before, he asked her how she was. Instead of speaking she started sucking and blowing on the stem adjacent to her mouth. Certain of the letter-containing squares on the screen by her bed lit up in succession. The typewriter on the table at the end of the bed clattered and what Angela wanted to say eventually appeared on a sheet of paper. She didn't bother with punctuation or capital letters.

'thank u 4 coming,' she typed.

Her eyes crinkled in what Stephen took to be an attempt at a smile.

'sorry cant talk soon wont breathe.'

'You heard the inquest verdict, did you?'

Stephen knew she had but could think of nothing else to say. The clattering of the typewriter started again and he followed each letter closely as it appeared on the paper.

'h's work in africa u have it.'

'No. I don't have it. I know nothing about it.'

The typewriter quickened.

'right in bottom drawer on left fetch.'

He walked over to one of the two chests of drawers in the left half of the room. The typewriter started up frantically again and he returned to the end of the bed and looked at the paper.

'other one.'

Stephen pulled open the bottom drawer. It was heavy with photograph albums, paperbacks, old exercise books and magazines. Angela had obviously just remembered what kind of mess the contents of the drawer were in because she resumed clattering. He returned to the typewriter.

'red notebook.'

He had to remove several objects before he found a red notebook at the back of the right-hand side of the drawer. He took it over to Angela, held it in front of her face and opened a few pages in succession. She closed her eyelids deliberately twice which Stephen took as affirmation that it was the right book. He recognised Henry Price's neat but sloping and nearly illegible writing. It seemed to be some kind of journal.

'make sure h gets credit dont trust the others.'

'Which others?'

'prof & r.'

'What had Henry been working on?'

'not sure i not medical african virus h v excited.'

The typewriter was getting slower and slower. Angela was exhausted. The doorbell rang and Richard Maynard's voice came through the speaker on the wall above her head.

'It's Richard. I've got the boys.'

Angela started one final laborious message.

'hide book destroy paper.'

Before she had finished the doorbell sounded again.

'Mummy, let us in. It's us. Mummy are you there?' an anxious child's voice came over the speaker.

The nurse came back into the room.

'Don't worry, Mrs. Price. I'll go downstairs and let them in.'

Stephen tore the sheet of paper out of the typewriter and stuffed it into his trouser pocket, but he hadn't quite finished putting in a new sheet when Richard entered the room with two red-haired boys in school uniform aged about twelve and fourteen. They glared at Stephen, walked solemnly over to the bed and said hello to their mother. The younger one kissed her on the cheek.

'Can we watch television, mum?' asked the younger.

Angela sucked and the television at the end of the bed erupted into life and the bedroom was completely taken over by the roaring and screeching of a car chase. The boys settled down on the double bed one on each side of their mother. Richard strode over to the chest of drawers, replaced all the bits and pieces Stephen had removed and pushed the bottom drawer shut. He cast a brief glance at the red notebook Stephen held in his left hand as he said goodbye to Angela. She shut her eyelids once and then crinkled her eyes.

Richard accompanied him downstairs. If he was put out by Stephen's presence, he concealed it well.

'I didn't expect to see you here, Stephen,' he said.

'I wasn't doing anything much this evening so I thought I'd pop round.'

'That's very nice of you.'

'Time must drag terribly for her just lying there.'

'She's getting to find visitors more and more tiring these days.'

'She seemed glad to see me,' Stephen countered.

'Was she able to say much today with her typewriter?'

It could have been a perfectly innocent question but Stephen felt he was fishing for something.

'Not much,' he replied.

'She seems to be rather preoccupied by something to do with Henry's work . . .'

Stephen changed the subject.

'Who's looking after the children at the moment?'

'I'd just been to fetch them. They're staying with Henry's parents in Kentish Town. They come over for about two hours every day. I'll be taking them back later in the evening.'

Richard opened the front door and Stephen made his way to his car. The temptation to look back at the house was even harder to resist than on his first visit. Somehow he managed to keep looking straight in front of him. He drove back to his flat in Stoke Newington as quickly as his rusting Allegro would allow. When he arrived home, he rushed upstairs without even seeing whether there was any mail for him. Once inside the flat he paused only to turn on the electric blow-heater and make himself a cup of coffee, before settling into the one armchair in the room and opening Henry's red notebook.

It was not an easy read. Most of the writing was in pencil and had faded. Even where it had not faded, Henry's flat sloping script was often little more than a wavy line. There was no flowing narrative and it appeared Henry had never read the notebook through nor corrected anything. Occasionally there was a jump of two or three months when nothing had been written. The journal started with the flight from Gatwick to Kampala in Uganda in early 1973. He described the stop-overs at Cairo and Khartoum and the problems of travelling by plane with two small children. Once the family had arrived in Kampala, he wrote of his misgivings about the ubiquitous and arbitrary soldiery. He mentioned the fears of the Asian professional and trade people. The journal then moved on to his work. It was clear that at that time Henry had nothing to do with rheumatology. His post at Makerere University was concerned mainly with virology both in a service and a research capacity. He also took clinics and he described how families would travel over a hundred miles and wait patiently for days outside the hospital to be seen. His particular research interest at that time were the African viral haemorrhagic fevers. The notebook included some brief notes on methods of assaying and extracting viral antigen and antibodies from serum. Henry took great pride in how he had managed to build up the virology services in the hospital. Together with an Indian engineer he developed a method of freezing virological specimens to below minus seventy degrees centigrade so that they would survive the long journeys from mission hospitals in remote country areas. It involved recharging a battery-driven refrigerator by connecting it to the alternator of a Land Rover: as long as you didn't run out of petrol and the Land Rover did not break down irretrievably the specimens reached Kampala unharmed. Angela Price also had a post at the university teaching English Literature; her pupils' favourites were Macbeth and King Lear. Meanwhile her children's books were beginning to sell well in England and she had been commissioned to write further stories. Altogether their life on the campus at Makerere seemed everything they could have wished for.

In the early part of 1975 Henry set off to north-western Uganda. The object of the trip was to make an epidemiological study of the people who lived on the banks of the Albert Nile north of Lake Albert and further west towards the border with Zaire. The idea was to take serum and determine the prevalence of various different virus infections. The area was about two hundred and fifty miles north-west of Kampala, but instead of going by the direct route which would have involved some punishing driving, it was decided to take the long way round by train. The Land Rovers – and spare alternators – were loaded on to the train at Kampala and the five-day long circuitous journey began. The first part of the journey was due east along the northern shores of Lake Victoria through Jinja-Bugembe in the opposite direction to their final destination. At Tororo, close to the border with Kenya, the train at last turned north. When Moale had been passed, the track began gradually to veer towards the west through Lira and Gulu to the north of Lake Kyoga. Eventually the Land Rovers were taken off the train at Pakwach on the west bank of the Albert Nile twenty miles north of Lake Albert. The next four months were spent travelling up and down the Nile as far as the Sudanese border, stopping at Mutir, Rhino Camp, Obongi and Laropi in the north. From these stopping places Henry drove into the hinterland towards Zaire, dispensing teeshirts and antibiotics at village clinics and taking blood specimens. He separated the serum and froze it. One particular trip took him to a place called Rigbo close to the Sudan. There and in the surrounding villages he found a remarkable number of patients with lymphopenia and a tumour known as Kaposi's sarcoma, which was endemic in the area but not usually seen in such numbers in one small place at one time. This clustering of cases led Henry to suspect an infectious and probably viral cause. He took seventy specimens of serum from the sufferers and labelled each one "Rigbo" with the date it was taken.

He returned to Kampala in September two months later than originally planned. This time he travelled overland. Although it was only about two hundred and fifty miles, the journey took four days. Several times the road was blocked by bands of soldiers, drunk with no officer in charge. On these occasions Sanu, the Indian virology technician, had to be hidden under a tarpaulin and boxes of medical supplies. The soldiers took anything that caught their fancy: antibiotics and syringes to sell on the black market, the Land Rovers' spare tyres and finally one of the Land Rovers themselves. At last Henry reached Makerere and was able to store his specimens more safely. But things had changed for the worse at the university. Asian doctors, technicians and administrative staff were being ousted from their jobs and an English professor of surgery, who protested, had been sacked too. What was happening on the campus was happening on a larger and more brutal scale in the city itself. Murder, rape and looting became increasingly commonplace. Communications and services deteriorated. In one of the ever more frequent power cuts Henry lost three quarters of the frozen specimens he had collected over three years. The telephones only occasionally worked and letters never came. The materials needed for work on those specimens which had not thawed in the power cuts never arrived. Henry and Angela finally decided to leave Uganda when Sanu was burnt alive by a mob who set fire to his father's paint shop. By paying five hundred pounds in bribes as well as the price of the tickets the family managed to get a flight back to England in the summer of 1976.

It was nearly midnight when Stephen came to the end of Henry Price's red notebook. The cup of coffee he had made three hours ago was untouched and a grey-brown scum had formed on the top. He made himself another cup and sat down again in the armchair. He knew what he had to do next. He went into the bedroom and looked under the bed where he kept back numbers of the "British Medical Journal." He cursed himself for not being the sensible, methodical type who filed his journals in chronological order and kept an alphabetical box-file of references of interesting articles. But he knew that one of those journals in that disorganised pile might confirm the nature of Henry's recent research. He carried the journals into the other room and stacked them at the foot of the armchair. He started to plough through them skimming the list of contents of each edition. Half an hour later, just when he was beginning to think he was on the wrong tack, he found what he was looking for, the paper that had made a dim and precarious impression on his memory bank. It was dated 4th August 1984:

"For Debate: AIDS : an Old Disease from Africa?"

CHAPTER EIGHT

There could be no other conclusion. Henry Price had been researching into the Acquired Immune Defiency Syndrome (AIDS). At some time in the past three years or so he must have realised that the epidemic he witnessed at Rigbo in 1975 had been an epidemic of AIDS. Was it possible that the samples of serum marked "Rigbo" had survived Idi Amin's holocaust and were now stored in one of the scores of deep-freeze units scattered across the hospital? AIDS had captured the medical research community's imagination as no other disease had for three decades. It had brought a new lease of life to scientific-based medicine, a chance to reassert its powers and silence the cavilling of sociologists, journalists, consumerists and the whole alternative medicine lobby. The stage was set for a classic man against the microbes battle and the names of the victors would have a place in history along with Pasteur, Koch, Fleming, Sabin and Salk.

Most of the important papers on AIDS had five or more authors. If Henry had been on the verge of an unprecedented breakthrough, how much more impressive that it was the work of one man working alone. But was it really likely that a forty-one year-old time-expired senior registrar in the rheumatology could succeed where the rest of the international AIDS industry had so far failed? There was only way to find out. The cardiology senior registrar with the instantly forgettable name had provided him with his starting point: the Virology Department.

But Stephen could not just march into the Virology Department and ask what Henry Price had been doing there. The head of the department was Dr. Devane. He was a kind, unworldly man with a genuine love of viruses – in particular those of the Herpes family – and watched their antics and progress with the fascination of a doting parent. His preoccupation with the academic side of his work explained why he had never been given a professorial chair. He had no time for committees and interdepartmental politics. It was Monday. Stephen looked up Virology in the hospital telephone directory and dialled Dr. Devane's extension.

'Devane here.'

'Good morning, Dr. Devane. My name is Stephen Hobbs. I'm the senior house officer in the Rheumatology Department.'

'Yes, Dr. Hobbs. What can I do for you?'

'Well, the thing is that in a few months' time I may have time for a research project . . . and one of the things I was thinking of looking at was the relationship between acute viral infections and the onset of rheumatoid arthritis.'

There was a pause before Dr. Devane spoke again.

'Hmmm. I see. It's a tangled subject. What particular aspect were you hoping to concentrate on?'

'That's what I was hoping I might be able to discuss with you.'

'I see . . . There has, as I am sure you're aware, been a fair amount of work done on this question but nothing conclusive has really emerged . . .'

'That's why I would greatly appreciate it if I could briefly sound you out on what is feasible and worth doing.'

'Of course, I would be delighted to talk to you. Are you free right now?'

'Would in half an hour's time be all right?'

'Fine, I'll see you then.'

Dr. Devane was an enthusiast. His hesitant response suggested that Stephen had not conjured up the most promising of pretexts for nosing around in the Virology Department. Obviously the viral origins of rheumatoid arthritis did not add up to a particularly auspicious research project. Stephen needed the half hour to go to the library and brush up on virological jargon so that he would not appear too implausible. He sat down at an empty desk in the library with a copy of the slim virology textbook which had enabled him to bluff his way through his final three years ago. He turned immediately to the chapter on the laboratory diagnosis of virus infection and scanned the pages in an effort to imprint the various techniques on his mind for the next hour. He filled his brain with tissue cultures, cytopathic effects, haemadsorption, immunofluorescence, neutralisation tests, electron microscopy, haemagglutination–inhibition, complement-fixation tests and the difference between IgG and IgM.

Thus armed he made his way to the Department of Virology, which was housed in a part of the hospital where Stephen had never ventured before. Instead of being in the pathology building, which had been erected many years before anyone had thought of viruses, the department consisted of a number of rooms wedged between Surgical Appliances and Hospital Security. In order to reach it Stephen had to leave the main hospital complex and cross a couple of narrow streets. If the style of building which contained the Department of Rheumatology could be described as 1930's municipal with a dash of Colditz castle, that of the Virology Department was unadulterated 1940's prefab. The building had never been intended as anything more than a temporary construction and had originally been the Tuberculosis Clinic. Stephen had first to pass Surgical Appliances before entering the virology laboratory. It was as cramped as the lab in the Rheumatology Department even though it operated as a service as well as a research lab.

'Excuse me,' Stephen asked one of the technicians, 'Could you tell me where I could find Dr. Devane's office, please?'

'He doesn't have an office,' came the reply.

At that moment the monkish wiry figure of Dr. Devane approached from the far end of the lab carrying two cups of coffee.

'Hello there,' he said, 'You must be Dr. Hobbs. Come and sit down over here.'

He led Stephen to one corner of the lab and put the cups down on the end of a lab bench which extended the whole length of one side of the room. He pulled up two high stools.

'Sit down, Dr. Hobbs.'

He pushed one of the cups of coffee towards Stephen.

'I hope you don't take sugar. We've run out.'

'No, that's fine. I don't,' Stephen lied.

'Good. Now tell me how you came to develop an interest in the aetiology of rheumatoid arthritis?'

Stephen had prepared an answer for this question.

'The main reason is that nearly every day for the past six months some patient or other has asked me what is the cause of their disease and I am tired of giving them the same old feeble reply . . .'

'Which is?'

'No one really knows but it is thought some environmental trigger, probably a virus, is responsible.'

'That's about as much as anyone can say at the moment. Even if the precipitating cause does turn out to be a virus, heredity, particularly the HLA antigen system, probably determines why some people are vulnerable and not others. It may not even be that a single virus is responsible – it may be that any one of a wide variety of viruses may initiate in genetically predisposed subjects an auto-immune process which finally results in damage to joint tissue. How do you propose to set about finding out?'

'I would start by looking at the material we get from all the new cases in the clinic – joint fluid, synovial biopsies and blood for serial antibodies.'

'Having first, of course, got advice from the epidemiologists about a suitable control group.'

'Of course. There would be two main strands to the work: the epidemiological and the virological.'

Stephen surprised himself with his capacity to bullshit. While they continued chatting about viral mechanisms of disease and how to study them, Dr. Devane showed him round the department. So irresistible was the virologist's enthusiasm that Stephen almost forgot his real reasons for being there and began to fantasize about going into research. Devane showed him the "Category 3 pathogen room" – more colloquially known as the "B 1 room" – where work was done on the most virulent organisms. Through the window of the heavy locked door Stephen watched the gloved and gowned technicians working with their hands inside a glass-fronted safety cabinet. Presumably this was where Henry Price did his research. Devane showed him where and how tissue cultures and viral isolates were stored: in ampoules or bottles stacked in incubators and fridges. It was possible that the essence of Henry's research was contained in a few small bottles.

Stephen was just about to leave when his bleep went off.

'May I use your phone, Dr. Devane?'

'Certainly. Go ahead.'

He dialled the switchboard and was put through to the caller.

'Ah, Stephen?'

'Yes?'

'It's Richard Maynard here. It's about your urethral swab.'

Dr. Devane was still standing next to Stephen.

'It's a bit difficult to talk at the moment . . . I'm in the middle of something.'

'I understand. There's no need for you to say anything. Just listen and I'll talk softly. Your swab has confirmed gonorrhoea but it's a resistant strain. You need a different antibiotic. Would you be able to come to the department some time later today?'

'Couldn't I just pick up a new prescription from the receptionist?'

'I'm afraid not. You need spectinomycin and that means an injection.'

'I see.'

'The best thing would be for you to come to the department at six this evening. The clinic will be over by then and everyone will have gone home. I'll give you the injection myself.'

He rang off before Stephen had a chance to say anything further. The idea of meeting Richard alone in a deserted building and receiving an injection filled him with unease.

'Trouble?' asked Devane with a benign smile.

'Oh, nothing in particular. I better be going now. Thankyou very much for talking to me, Dr. Devane.'

'It's a pleasure. What I suggest you do is first go and have a good look at the literature and see whether you can develop any promising ideas. Then draw up a protocol and come and discuss it again in detail.'

Stephen had still not achieved what he had come for. He decided to risk a frontal assault.

'I believe Dr. Price was doing some research in your lab before he died.'

'Yes. Poor Henry. Terrible business, wasn't it?'

'He was my senior registrar. I never knew until recently that he had an interest in virology. He kept very quiet about it.'

'I hardly ever saw him in the lab during daytime. He did most of his work at night. Kept extraordinary hours especially just recently. The reason he kept so quiet about it was that he didn't want David Carling to know what he was up to. I'm not sure why. I can't really see David objecting. I used to tease him about his secrecy, but he was absolutely adamant that he didn't want his research to be bandied about.'

'He was interested in tropical infections, wasn't he? I gather he spent a few years in Africa in the early 'seventies.'

'That's right. He had a collection of serum from his time out there and was using it to propagate virus in tissue culture.'

'You mean there was live virus in the serum and he had found a way of growing it in the lab?'

'Yes. He could grow it ad infinitum. It was an elegant piece of work. He knew his stuff all right. It's just a pity he wasn't employing his talents on something a little less obscure than the African Haemorrhagic Fevers.'

Stephen was not sure what to make of what Dr. Devane was saying. Had Henry actually been working on the African Viral Haemorrhagic Fevers rather than AIDS? Or had he concealed the true nature of his work? Or was Devane lying?

'Had he written up any of his research?' asked Stephen.

'No. I kept telling him he should. But he was too impatient. He seemed to want to press on further before committing anything to print. He had at least enough material for several papers. But now we will never know exactly what he achieved unless he left some kind of written record.'

'He wasn't working with anyone else then?'

'Certainly not closely. Though on a couple of occasions he did bring someone down to the lab. I can't remember his name . . . had an earring in his ear – that I do remember. Is it meant to signify anything?'

'What?'

'An earring.'

'I think it depends which side it's on.'

'Really. Is that a fact?'

'I don't think I could go so far as to say it's a fact.'

'Anyway, it seems a great shame Henry's work will never see the light of day.'

'Couldn't someone take on where he left off?'

'Very difficult without access to Henry's lab notes – if he kept any.'

'So his tissue cultures are still in the lab?'

'Yes. I expect so.'

Devane turned to one of the technicians and asked where Henry's tissue cultures were kept. He was directed to a fridge just inside the "Category 3 pathogen room". He and Stephen donned gowns and gloves, unlocked the door and went in. Immediately inside the door to the left was a five-foot high refrigerator with a small compartment at the top and a larger one below. The technician had followed them. They turned in response to her tapping on the window in the door and saw her point at the top compartment. Dr. Devane reached up and opened the top door of the fridge.

'Let's see what we have here.'

There was one group of bottles on the left and another on the right. He pulled down each bottle in turn and inspected the labelling.

'That's strange. None of these seem to be Henry's'

Devane turned again to the door. 'Not here,' he shouted shaking his head exaggeratedly to the technician on the other side of the window. She looked surprised, shrugged her shoulders and pointed to the lower part of the fridge. With some difficulty Devane pulled the lower door open. There were no bottles or ampoules to be seen. There would have been no room for any bottles, even if anyone had wanted to store some there. The whole compartment was filled by a frozen figure in jeans and anorak curled up in the foetal position. The face was a bloodless yellow-white. It was Eileen the habitual overdoser.

*　　　*　　　*

While they were waiting for the police, Stephen talked to the technicians. They could think of no reason why anyone should have needed to open the fridge in the last week. Recently it had only contained three separate cultures. Apart from Henry Price's which was now missing, one belonged to a research fellow who had been away on holiday and the other had not been used for six months. The bottom half of the fridge had not been opened for over a year. When no else was looking, Stephen reached down and picked up a piece of paper lying scrumpled up on the floor of the fridge adjacent to Eileen's foot. It tore – or rather broke – leaving a frozen portion firmly adjerent to her shoe. It was impossible to unravel the paper without tearing it further. He looked through the window in the door of the "category 3 pathogen room" and, seeing that the police had arrived, he stuffed the fragment into his trouser pocket.

Stephen was relieved to see that it was not the same policeman who attended at Henry Price's death. A plain-clothes man had been sent, a lanky man whose spine curved forward like a banana and ended in a disproportionately small balding head that poked out of the collar of his black leather jacket like the head of a tortoise. After a few words with Devane, who helped him put on gown and gloves, the detective was shown into the "B 1 room". He stooped down, looked into the lower compartment of the fridge and then glanced at the catch on the door.

'Does anyone know who she is?' he asked.

'Her name is Eileen Pearce,' replied Stephen.

'You know her then?'

'She's a St. Nathaniel's regular. Every junior hospital doctor knows her. I must have seen her four or five times in casualty myself.'

'Is that a syringe poking out from her fist?'

'It looks like it, yes.'

'How long might she have been here?'

'As far as we know.' answered Devane, 'the last time the top part of the fridge was opened was about one week ago. As for the bottom part no one has any idea.'

'The last time I saw her alive,' added Stephen,' was six evenings ago when she came in with another overdose.'

Stephen suppressed an urge to tell how Eileen had walked out of the Casualty Department that evening saying she was going to search for Henry Price's killer. The desire to unsettle the complacency of the St. Nathaniel's establishment only just gave way to the need to keep Henry's AIDS secret.

'Did she regularly shoot drugs?' the detective asked Stephen.

'She'd shoot them, swallow them, sniff them, do anything she could to get them into her system.'

The detective walked round the small room inspecting its sparse functional fittings. He stopped at the safety cabinet. He put both his arms into the sleeves which stretched through the glass front into the cabinet's working area.

'What's this for?'

'It's a safety cabinet,' explained Devane. 'In order to handle specimens you put your gloved hands through the sleeves.'

'What sort of work's done in this room?'

'This is where we handle the most virulent viruses: lassa fever, smallpox, that sort of thing.'

The policeman hastily removed his arms from the sleeves.

'You mean there's smallpox and lassa fever in here?' he said alarmed.

'No. I was only joking. They're category 4 pathogens. We only keep category 3 – Hepatitis B, recombinant viruses and so on. I'll show you.'

Devane walked back to the fridge and opened the upper compartment.

'That's quite all right, sir. That won't be necessary. Perhaps we could continue our discussion outside.'

'It's really quite safe,' said Devane waving a tissue culture bottle up and down as though trying to gauge it's weight. 'And the room's quite secure.'

'Then how did she get in here?'

'I really have no idea,' the virologist replied.

The dectective was anxious to leave the room and tried unsuccessfully to open the door.

'How do we get out of here?' he asked.

'Allow me.'

Devane opened the door and the three of them walked out, took off their gowns and gloves and placed them in a plastic laundry bag which was destined to be incinerated.

'Can I get you some coffee?' he asked the detective. 'I'm afraid it will have to be black. We've just finished off the last of the milk. Oh yes, and the sugar's run out too.'

The offer of Virology Department coffee held no appeal for the policeman and he bent down to look closely at the lock of the "category 3 pathogen room" door. He took a wallet out of his inside jacket pocket and produced a credit card, which he manoeuvred between the latch and the door-frame. A few tweaks of the card were all that was required to open the door. He uncurled his spine and turned round to look down at Dr. Devane.

'I suggest you review your security, sir. The Crime Prevention Department of the Metropolitan Police are always pleased to advise.'

'But who on earth would want to break into the "B 1 room"?'

The detective shrugged. Stephen shrugged too but his mind was on theft. Dishonesty was not unheard of as the handmaiden of ambition in academic circles. The most blatant examples were downright fraud, the faking or even the invention of results. Plagiarism was less rare. Commonest of all were the people who schemed to get their names added to papers to which they had contributed nothing, and some professors thought little of taking over the promising projects of their underlings while diverting them to work of less potential. Stephen's disenchantment with teaching hospital medicine made it easy for him to imagine that someone might have coveted Henry Price's research enough to steal. It was only one more small step to start entertaining the notion of murder again. Stephen's physical and mental tiredness vanished, routed by the strong reviving brew of conspiracy and murder.

'I would be most grateful, sir,' the detective asked Devane, 'if you and Dr. Hobbs would kindly give us a statement about how you found the body.'

'Certainly,' Devane replied.

'We would also like to interview all the laboratory staff. It would greatly help if you could close the laboratory for the rest of the day.'

'Impossible. We have specimens coming in all the time.'

It was clear from the policeman's expression that he meant what he said.

'I'm sorry but they'll just have to be stored and left until tomorrow. It'll be a while before we can remove the body. She's frozen hard. We'll have to wait till she's defrosted sufficiently to move.'

'You're saying that the fridge will have to be turned off?'

'I'm afraid so, sir. We can't leave her there, can we?'

'But what about the specimens in the fridge? They'll be ruined.'

'I'm sorry but there's no alternative. There'll have to be a Coroner's post mortem.'

'Right,' said Devane testily, 'we'll just have to find another fridge then.'

The virologist turned away and walked determinedly across to the other side of the laboratory. After a few words with one of the technicians, a small fridge was found and brought to the "B 1 room". Devane regowned and took it into the room with the help of the technician. Making no attempt to conceal his annoyance at the disruption of his department, he pulled out the plug of the large fridge. One by one he pointedly removed each tissue culture bottle and placed them in the smaller fridge. When he came out again he turned to the policeman.

'I would advise your men to take extreme care when they remove the body.'

'Of course, sir.'

'There's something else you ought to know,' said Stephen. 'Eileen Pearce had Hepatitis B.'

'What's that?' asked the detective.

'It means,' Devane chipped in with satisfaction, 'that she has serum hepatitis and that her remains must be handled with extreme caution to avoid the infection being transmitted. It also means that the pathologists may well refuse to perform an autopsy.'

Either the virologist was displaying the other side of his usually benign nature – the academic snob intolerant of the demands of the outside world – or he was faintly mad and really held the police responsible for the inconvenience to which he had been put. Either way Stephen felt a little sorry for the detective and the police in general. He supposed they must be on the receiving end of rudeness and hostility more than any other profession. By the time he had finished giving his statement, he realised that it was nearly two o'clock and he had not stepped on to the ward yet that day. It was high time he saw what Paul Goss had been up to.

Paul was gaining confidence and beginning to become a little cocky. He had admitted four emergency cases that day without having to call for help. He took Stephen first to the Coronary Care Unit to see the first admission of the day, a bank manager who commuted from Walton-on-Thames and had collapsed at Waterloo Station. He lay anxiously on the cardiac bed, his back supported at an angle of forty-five degrees and his body chained to an E.C.G. monitor. Fortunately his coronary was a mild one and there were no complications. The rest of the admissions were to Ward 3A: an acute asthma, a kidney infection and an eighty year-old in heart failure. Their condition was also stable. Stephen was just about to leave when he saw Reg Dicks at the far end of the ward talking to a patient.

'Who's that patient Resus Reggie's talking to?'

'Mr. Howard,' replied Paul. 'You remember – that chap Reggie resuscitated by D.C. shock in casualty last week.'

'I didn't think he had any interest in conscious patients.'

'He always comes and talks to his successes.'

'So that's how he gets his kicks.'

'What do you mean?'

'By lapping up the gratitude of the patients he's resuscitated and making sure they know he was the one responsible.'

'That's a bit unfair, isn't it, Stephen?'

'Do you know of a better explanation?'

Paul Goss was obviously better disposed towards Dr. Dicks.

'Yes. It happens to be his research project.'

'Research project?'

'It's his own personal research. Apparently he has no sanction from the Anaesthetics Department for what he's doing.'

'Well, don't keep me in suspense any longer, Paul. What is it he's researching into?'

'Death.'

'What do you mean "death"?'

'Not exactly "death", more the state that exists between cardio-respiratory arrest and a successful resuscitation.'

'You mean all that endless rolling green meadows and glowing light at the end of the tunnel stuff?' Stephen snorted.

'Something like that, yes.'

'Hardly scientific, is it?'

'It's not meant to be. His interest is theological.'

'You're joking.'

'No. I'm not. It's the after-life he's interested in. Didn't you know he's God-squad?'

'Reg Dicks God-squad! I don't believe it.'

'All right, don't believe it. But just go and ask anyone in the Anaesthetics Department. Why do you think they call him "Resurrection Reggie"?'

'I didn't know they did.'

'It's true. I promise.'

'But he's nothing like the rest of the St. Nathaniel's God-squad.'

'They won't have anything to do with him. Too extreme even for them. Look, we better get a move on, Stephen, or we'll be late for the Contemporary Topics in Medicine seminar.'

'You carry on, Paul. I'm sure you'll find it very edifying. I'd rather have some lunch. I gave those seminars up months ago. What's it on this time?'

'AIDS.'

*   *   *

Stephen was desperate for food but he could not pass up the opportunity to find out who at St. Nathaniel's was interested in AIDS. When he and Paul entered the lecture theatre it became clear that nearly everyone had an interest in AIDS. It was unusual for there to be more than about fifty people attending the Contemporary Topics in Medicine seminar but today the lecture theatre was full. They only just managed to find two seats at the back of the auditorium. Nearly all the consultants were there including most of the surgeons who were not renowned for attendance at academic meetings. There was a bevy of senior nursing officers which was also unusual. Totally unprecedented was the presence of the shop stewards of N.U.P.E. and C.O.H.S.E. who represented the technicians and ancillary workers. But as yet there was no speaker even though it was five minutes past three.

'Who's supposed to be giving the talk?' Stephen asked Paul.

'Some new consultant from the clap department.'

The audience were showing signs of restlessness. Another minute passed and still no one appeared to conduct the seminar. Mr. Hardcastle-Phelps, the vascular surgeon, rose from his seat in the middle of the second row, coughed loudly and looked at his watch. With clearly audible "excuse me's" he made his way to the end of the row. He walked to the front of the auditorium, paused to look ostentatiously again at his watch and swept out through the swing-doors. Still no speaker arrived and the level of noise in the lecture theatre quickly grew from whispers to a hubbub of general conversation. Stephen became aware of a dampness at the top of his left thigh. He put his hand into his trouser pocket and retrieved the thawed piece of paper he found at the bottom of the "category 3 pathogen room" refrigerator taking as much care as possible not to tear it. It eventually came out as three soggy separate pieces. He did his best to smooth them out and fit them together. The ink had faded and run where it was not smudged. Although it was totally illegible, the sloping writing was unmistakably that of Henry Price.

The lecture theatre doors suddenly swung open and the auditorium hushed. The speaker had arrived. It was Richard Maynard. It had never occurred to Stephen that Richard might be a consultant. To use a piece of hospital slang dear to students and junior hospital doctors there was nothing "consultoid" about his appearance. Stephen could never bring himself to address any consultant as "sir", but for anyone so to have called Richard Maynard would have been totally incongruous. He had no gravitas, the hair on his temples had not even begun to turn silver; at work he always wore corduroy and desert boots. He looked as though he had never possessed a single club or old boy's tie, let alone ever worn one. But he did know enough to turn up at the Coroner's court in a dark suit. Most Englishmen can make a reasonable stab at guessing the social background of another Englishman, but with Richard even the best exponents of this guessing game would be flummoxed. In that, he rather resembled Reg Dicks who was sitting as usual at one end of the second row of the lecture theatre. After meeting Richard in the "Special Clinic" Stephen had looked him up in the "Medical Directory". He was not a product of Oxbridge or any of the London teaching hospitals. He had not even been trained at Edinburgh, Glasgow or St. Andrew's. He was a graduate of one of the newer medical schools in the Midlands: a rarity indeed among the consultant body of St. Nathaniel's. His membership of the Royal College of Physicians had been obtained within two and a half years of qualifying and he had then spent two years in America in Baltimore where he had obtained a Ph.D on the subject of gut infections in the homosexual male. He returned to a senior registrarship in a department of genito-urinary medicine on Merseyside before moving to St. Nathaniel's. His list of publications was extensive.

Richard Maynard apologised for being late but gave no reason. In the front few rows the congregated consultants did little to put him at ease. Some folded their arms and stared at him fixedly. Others slouched gazing at the ceiling and barely stifling their yawns. "Percy" Pritchard the urologist, also assistant dean and Justin Rugwood's father-in-law, studied the racing tips in "The Sporting Life". The consultants of St. Nathaniel's were a difficult bunch to impress at the best of times but Stephen had never before sensed such a collective hostility towards one of their number. Was it simply that the man looked like a television producer and had a stud in his ear? Or was it jealousy? For years Venereology had been a Cinderella subject, almost an outcast from the mainstream of medicine. But now – thanks to the promiscuity of homosexuals – it was at the forefront of academic medicine grabbing the headlines in the national newspapers as well as the scientific journals.

Richard spoke without notes and without slides. He started diffidently and quietly. Too quietly. He had hardly uttered one sentence when a voice near the back of the auditorium shouted to him to speak up. A brief flash of anger, not embarrassment, caused his face to colour. It was obviously not the first time he had been confronted by the hostility of the St. Nathaniel's establishment. He started his talk again.

'In case there is anyone here who has been living on the planet Mars or who has not opened a medical journal or even a newspaper for the past few years, the acronym "AIDS" stands for the Acquired Immune Deficiency Syndrome. Contrary to popular belief it is not a syndrome which only affects homosexuals, heroin addicts and a few luckless Haitians and haemophiliacs. In Africa, where the condition is likely to have originated, the incidence is confined to heterosexuals. In the western world, though first recognised in the gay community, it is increasingly being seen in heterosexuals also.'

Richard's frosty reception was beginning to work to his advantage. The anger it had roused had given a conciseness and attack to his talk. Over the next half an hour he gave an unfaltering and lucid account which offered the audience no opportunity for sabotage. Finally he moved on to the work being done at St. Nathaniel's.

'At St. Nathaniel's we have now dealt with approximately fifty cases of AIDS, of which a little over one half have died. Despite the development of anti-viral drugs, there is no prospect of an effective cure in the next few years. The best hope for the immediate future lies in prevention. The two medical advances likely to occur in the next year or two are the development of a reliable test for the carrier state of AIDS and secondly the development of a vaccine. The Genito-Urinary Department at St. Nathanial's are involved in research in both areas and we hope to be making an important announcement in the near future.'

The obvious question what that announcement might be did not materialise from the audience. Bottoms shifted and coughs were coughed while the consultants of St. Nathaniel's groped hard to think of deflating comments. None came. The silence became awkward. Heads began to turn round and scan the auditorium for potential questioners. But Richard Maynard was not embarrassed. The silence from the first few rows constituted a small victory, a signal that he was winning this particular contest. Partly to end the silence and partly because he could not resist asking, Stephen stood up and spoke.

'Dr. Maynard, I would like to ask about the latency between infection with the HTLV-III virus and the full clinical manifestation of AIDS.'

'That's a good question and I'm afraid my answer must necessarily be vague. The latency period appears to be variable. In some cases it may be as short as a few months. In other cases it is considerably longer.'

'Could it be as long as years?'

Richard paused before answering and pursed his lips slightly without removing his gaze from Stephen at the back of the room.

'How many years had you in mind?' he asked as though it were a strange question.

'You mentioned it is probable that AIDS has been occuring in Central Africa for many years. Would it be possible for a European to have become infected as long as eight or nine years ago and not have developed AIDS until some time in the last six months or so?'

'What evidence there is would suggest it would not be impossible but unlikely.'

Stephen had one more question.

'Does the mode of transmission of the virus affect the latency period in any way?'

'You mean is the latency different in homosexuals, intravenous drug abusers or haemophiliacs? That again cannot be answered with complete confidence. But as far as we know it makes little difference.'

Stephen sat down. After a pause of about ten seconds Mrs. Wand, the Senior Nursing Officer, stood up. She was a tall, thin woman in her early forties with too much make-up and blond-streaked hair. She read from a piece of paper.

'The Royal College of Nursing is concerned that by the end of the century the number of AIDS patients will reach several hundred thousand if it continues to spread at the present rate. Nurses are obviously first in line to be infected by body fluids from these patients. If we are to nurse them in ever increasing numbers, we must be given firm assurances it is safe to do so.'

'Where did you get the figure of several hundred thousand from?' asked Richard.

Mrs. Wand was taken aback. She had not expected the question to be thrown back at her.

'From a report,' she replied.

'Who were the authors of this report? Can you give me a reference?'

'I don't have the exact reference at my finger tips but the Royal College of Nursing in a recent statement said . . .'

'I know exactly what they have said and I have been trying for some time to find out where these figures come from. With the greatest of respect this estimate of the future prevalence of AIDS is based on the assumption that the incidence will increase geometrically each year up until the year 2000. That is simply not tenable.'

'But you wouldn't deny,' continued Mrs. Wand having recovered some of her composure, 'that whatever the correct figures may be AIDS is increasing at an alarming rate and nurses are increasingly at risk?'

Before Richard could answer, the nattily dressed and brown-touped figure of Mr. Ray Daniels, shop steward and operating theatre technician, rose to his feet.

'It's time to stop beating about the bush,' he began. 'At the end of the day the real truth is that all hospital workers are at risk. Unless management gives proper assurances, we will have no choice but to withdraw our services from the patients in question. It is obligatory that the workers in this hospital are at all times consulted about the presence and movement of AIDS patients, and they must be informed who these patients are and where they are being seen or admitted in the hospital.'

'You're suggesting that the members of your union should be given a list of in- and out-patients suffering from AIDS?' asked Richard.

'That is what my members are demanding, yes.'

'What about the patients' confidentiality?'

'My concern is for my members' safety.'

'In my talk I took pains to put into perspective the danger of contracting AIDS among those who are not in the main groups at risk. HTLV-III does not behave like the common cold virus. You can't catch it from the person sitting next to you on the bus. You can't catch it by standing in the breeze from Camden Town. In this country there has only been one recorded case of hospital personnel infecting themselves, and this was by accidentally pricking their finger with a contaminated needle. But because the nurse in question had no other risk factors she never went on to develop AIDS, even though tests proved that infection had taken place.'

Richard had at last given his adversaries an opening. "Percy" Pritchard took the opportunity without even looking up from his "Sporting Life".

'But for a while she may have become that dangerous creature, the symptomless carrier of AIDS capable of spreading the virus to unsuspecting people who fall outside the usual groups at risk. You yourself mentioned it was becoming seen increasingly among heterosexuals.' He then looked up from his paper and stared straight at Richard. 'You can't have it both ways. You can't go on saying what a serious and increasing health problem AIDS is becoming, and then in the next breath say there isn't any need for the general public to get worried. And surely a nurse carrying the infection would be a hazard to patients whose resistance to infection has been lowered by other disease, which in contrast to AIDS is no fault of their own?'

'It is certainly true,' replied Richard without all his earlier assuredness, 'that AIDS will soon become a major public health concern and that there is still much work to be done on its mode of transmission in the community. But as far as hospital personnel are concerned, all the evidence points to the risks of infection being less than with serum hepatitis. Compared with smoking, drinking alcohol and driving a car, the risks are minimal.'

'But,' Mr. Pritchard continued, 'smoking, drinking and driving are things we choose to do ourselves. Hospital personnel cannot be expected to welcome even the slightest risk of catching the self-inflicted diseases of minority groups.'

Even from the back of the auditorium Stephen could sense the wave of satisfaction rippling along the front few rows of the audience.

'I would like to make a minor comment on some of the terms used this afternoon.' A faintly audible groan arose from several different parts of the lecture theatre. It was Dr. Dyson, the chest physician and St. Nathaniel's oldest consultant, whose chief delight for many years had been correcting medical students' use of English. 'Many may regard it as pedantic to quibble about words. But sloppy usage leads to sloppy thinking. I refer to the phrase "gay community". The word "community" has been debased by being applied arbitrarily to any grouping of people. Thus we no longer talk about Sikhs but the "Sikh community". We no longer talk about miners but the "mining community". I have even heard of the homeless being called the "homeless community". But why do we never hear of the "auburn-haired community" or the "left-handed community"? Because the word "community" has become a piece of verbal sleight of hand. It is used to convey the existence of a unity of sentiments and interests among a given collection of individuals which in reality exists only in the mind of the speaker. The fault is further compounded in the expression "gay community". The use of the word "gay" to denote homosexual has robbed the language of a perfectly good word which has no exact equivalent. Its use renders ludicrous some of the finest passages of English poetry. Personally I do not like the word "homosexual" either and prefer the more accurate "homosexualist"'.

Dr. Dyson sat down with the kind of expression on his face which would suggest that his speech had been greeted with rapturous applause. He seemed impervious to the indifferent silence that followed. Richard clearly did not wish to continue this line of debate and glanced systematically at each part of the audience in search of the next questioner. Eventually Dr. Herman, St. Nathaniel's first professor of general practice, decided to have his say.

'Dr. Maynard, I am right – am I not? – that you said about fifty patients with AIDS had been seen at this hospital?'

'That's right.'

'Does this mean that St. Nathaniel's has seen more patients with AIDS than any other hospital in Britain?'

'Yes.'

'The local press and many patients in the area are starting to refer to St. Nathaniel's as "the AIDS hospital". This is causing considerable concern among local G.P.'s as more and more patients are refusing to be referred here.'

'Have you any figures, Professor Herman, for the number of patients declining referral to St. Nathaniel's because of our work on AIDS?' asked Richard.

Dr. Herman's bland face creased into a mildly admonitory but tolerant smile.

'Of course I haven't. But I can assure you the issue is constantly being raised at local G.P. meeings. The fact that patients' attitudes are not entirely rational in no way diminishes the very real strength of feeling that exists.'

"Percy" Pritchard had never acknowledged the need for a professor of general practice and was pleasantly surprised that such a person could have anything worthwhile to contribute.

'Professor Herman,' he interrupted, 'and his colleagues in general practice are quite right to be concerned. I'm sure I am speaking for all the consultants in this hospital in expressing a fear that any further expansion of the facilities for AIDS patients may lead to fewer patients being referred to us.'

'Are you talking about your National Health or your private patients, Mr. Pritchard?' asked Richard.

The auditorium hushed completely and the atmosphere suddenly intensified. The whole audience strained to see Pritchard's expression and catch his next words.

'I would have thought, Dr. Maynard, that even though you have only been at this hospital for one year, you would by now have learnt of the long tradition at St. Nathaniel's of making no distinction between private and National Health patients.'

Stephen could not imagine how the seminar could deteriorate any further. But he had reckoned wihout Owen Hesketh-Jones who was sitting in the fifth row with Gwynneth Morgan at his side. He stood up and addressed the meeting in his loud totally self-assured baritone.

'Being a simple-minded surgeon who wouldn't know an antigen from an antibody, the solution to the AIDS problem seems to me pretty straightfoward. The key is prevention and the responsibility lies with the patients themselves. If homosexuals would simply stop putting their members into each others' rectums, they would not only be doing themselves – but the rest of us as well – a huge favour.'

A few half-stifled titters came from among the ranks of medical students at the back of the auditorium followed by some low mumbling. This state of affairs was soon ended by Professor Hamish.

'I have listened to this afternoon's proceedings in amazement. Amazement that a discussion at one of the best known teaching hospitals in Britain of a newly described disease of immense scientific and social importance could have provoked not the spirit of enquiry but a display of self-interest and boorishness. For God's sake what are we? Are we some kind of latter-day inquisition? Or are we doctors? This hospital was founded as a charitable institution open to all comers including the victims of an earlier plague, the Black Death. Since when has it been the prerogative of doctors to make judgements on the life-style of their patients? The simple truth is that patients with AIDS are sick like any other. This hospital happens to be in an area where AIDS is relatively common and the problem is not going to go away simply because we don't like it. St. Nathaniel's is at the forefront of creative research in this area and in the near future this research could soon help to put the hospital back on the international map as a research institution.'

Before Hamish had finished, "Percy" Pritchard stood up and tucking his "Sporting Life" under his arm left the lecture theatre. The rest of the consultants were not slow to follow. Once the front five rows had emptied, Richard Maynard took the opportunity to make his escape and gradually the rest of the audience made their way out through the swing-doors and returned to the less acrimonious business of seeing to patients.

CHAPTER NINE

The next two hours were spent with Paul Goss on Ward 3A. To Stephen's disappointment Sally Mason was not on duty that afternoon. After two cups of tea and six digestive biscuits he felt strong enough to go round the ward. Although Stephen had to force himself to concentrate on the task at hand, he and Paul saw every patient and checked their progress and response to treatment with more than usual thoroughness. It was as though he was not sure when or if he would next be able to go on a ward round, and he was therefore making as sure as he could that every loose end had been taken care of. Much as he had rooted for Richard Maynard in his confrontation with the St. Nathaniel's establishment in the seminar, he approached the impending appointment and injection at the "Special Clinic" with a deep sense of unease. Everything pointed to Maynard being the most likely person to benefit from appropriating Henry's research.

A little after six, Stephen left the main hospital and made his way to the Department of Genito-Urinary Medicine. Everything in that part of the city closed at five o'clock and as no one actually lived in the area, the streets were completely deserted. The only sign of life came from "The Apple and Pears". The silhouettes of the drinkers could just be made out through the frosted-glass windows. He tried to guess the identity of each silhouette. Above the uninterrupted jabber of off-duty doctors and nurses telling the same old anecdotes and exchanging the same old gossip only the voice of Owen-Hesketh-Jones was recognisable. 'Why do I keep going in there?' thought Stephen as he walked past the pub, 'I don't even like many of the regulars who drink there.' But despite everything on his mind he had to make a conscious effort to turn away from its warmth and resist its languid magnetism.

He reached Bodkin Street where the "Special Clinic" found its home. The street's one streetlight was not working and he paused to get his bearings. He could make out little in front of him except the mist of his own breath. But Bodkin Street was only about fifty yards long and he remembered the main entrance to the clinic being half way down on the right. When he reached the clinic, he pushed open its outer and then its inner glass door and went in. It was deserted and the only source of illumination downstairs was the fitful flickering of the faulty strip lighting behind the reception desk at the far end of the foyer.

'Hallo. Is anyone there?' he said in little more than a whisper. He cleared his throat and tried again more loudly and with a greater show of confidence. 'Dr. Maynard, are you there?'

The only sound was a faint electronic humming from upstairs. Stephen climbed the stairs. At the top he found himself in an unlit corridor. At the end of the corridor a line of greenish light issued feebly from a door that was only a few inches open. The light was not enough to show where the light-switches were. He walked slowly and as quietly as he could down the corridor, his hand groping unsuccessfully along the wall for a light-switch. The humming was coming from the same door as the greenish light. After what seemed an age he at last reached the door and pulled it open. It led to a small laboratory with a bench, a safety cabinet and several fridges and incubators. He opened one of the fridges and saw several rows of tissue cultures. At the end of the laboratory was a "category 3 pathogen room" which like the one in the Virology Department contained a large refrigerator. The door was locked. Stephen tried to remember how the detective had opened Dr. Devane's "B 1 room" door. He took out his one and only credit card and wedged it into the latch. He slid and wiggled it in every direction. Nothing happened. He tried again with more force. Just as his Barclaycard snapped into two pieces, he thought he heard the downstairs doors clatter open and shut. Complete silence followed and then a few quick footsteps and once again silence. Stephen began to panic and felt as though his heart were trying to batter its way through the front of his chest. He must be mad. He was alone and creeping around an unlit building waiting to receive an injection from a man he believed capable of theft and possibly even murder. Entry through the front door might work for 007 but what chance did Stephen Hobbs have? There was nowhere to hide. He looked round for an escape route. There was none.

He even scanned the walls of the lab for the kind of grille or hatch to a ventilator shaft which had so often saved Bond's and the civilised world's bacon. The only hope was to get downstairs to the main doors. He edged out again into the corridor closing the lab door as softly as he could. It was pitch dark and for several seconds he stood absolutely still. Suddenly the silence was broken by a few more rapid footsteps from downstairs and then a sound like the main doors being locked. With the absurd hope that he might be able to pass the owner of the footsteps he started to edge along the wall of the corridor in the direction of the stairs. The footsteps were softer now but appeared to be coming up the stairs towards him very slowly. With each step could be heard a little grunt of effort. Stephen was just beginning to think the best policy might be to make a mad dash downstairs and hurl himself through the glass doors like a stuntman, when a light-switch three feet in front of him snapped on. The approaching figure let out a terrified high-pitched scream, tottered backwards nearly losing its balance and dropping an ancient British Airways travel bag to the ground. Through his half-closed dazzled eyes Stephen made out the shocked white face of Dr. Devane. They stared at each other speechless for a few seconds. The virologist looked old, haggard and strained compared with his usual animated self. The expression of donnish enthusiasm and quiet amusement had left his eyes; it made him look more than his sixty years. Instead of his usual sprightly and erect posture his shoulders had slumped into an attitude of defeat and exhaustion. He was the first to speak.

'Dr. Hobbs. Good God, you gave me fright. I thought the place was empty. Do you make a habit of wandering round dark deserted buildings at night?'

'I couldn't find the light-switch,' replied Stephen. 'I was trying to find Dr. Maynard.'

'He isn't here then?'

'It seems not.'

'You've tried the door at the end of the corridor, have you?'

Before Stephen could answer, Devane set off down the corridor and opened the door to the lab. Stephen followed him into the room. The virologist became more agitated as he walked round the lab. He opened each of the fridges in turn and impatiently inspected their contents before making his way to the "category 3 pathogen room". He tried the door unsuccessfully and then picked up one half of the broken Barclaycard from the latch and the other half from where it had dropped on to the floor. He took a close look at the credit card, sighed and shrugged his shoulders despairingly. He turned to Stephen.

'This seems to be yours,' he said handing over the card. He seemed to expect an explanation but Stephen gave none and simply put the Barclaycard into his pocket. 'You ought to be more careful where you leave it. You never know who might pick it up.' Stephen could still think of nothing to say. 'You're more interested in Henry Price than the viral aetiology of rheumatoid arthritis, aren't you?'

'I think someone has stolen his research,' Stephen finally spoke not at all sure it was a wise thing to say. 'Whatever he told you I don't think his work had anything to do with the African viral haemorrhagic fevers.'

'I seem to be the only person completely in the dark about what that man had been up to. And it was my lab he was using too . . . and with my blessing. Henry Price has caused me more trouble than all the setbacks of the past ten years put together.'

'What do you mean?'

'He was the reason that girl was found dead in the department. And indirectly he is the reason the lab is going to be closed.'

'Closed? But Why?'

'Closed pending the results of an inquiry into the standards of safety and security.'

'When did that happen?' asked Stephen getting more and more lost.

'This afternoon. The powers that be – the administrators, the board of governors, the Department of Health and Social Security, and God knows who else – they have decided. Not only had that girl been able to get into the "B 1 room", but she was riddled with AIDS. And to cap it all she appears to have overdosed by dissolving heroin in fluid from a tissue culture bottle and then injecting herself.'

'But what has all that got to do with Henry Price? He died several days before she did.'

'If it hadn't been for him, she would have chosen somewhere else to kill herself.'

'I'm sorry. I don't understand.'

'He introduced her to the Virology Department. He asked me if he could see the occasional patient in the department and like a fool I said yes.'

'But why see her there? Why see her at all? How do you know he was doing what you say?'

'Here. I've dug these out from the records office downstairs.'

Dr. Devane opened his travel bag and handed over a file. On the front cover was Eileen Pearce's name; in larger letters was printed "The Department of Genito-Urinary Medicine". Inside Stephen found several entries, all except the first written in Henry Price's writing.

'His research was on AIDS,' continued Devane, 'wasn't it?'

'I'm almost certain. Yes.' Stephen replied.

'And that's what you were after in the "B 1 room"? But what good would it do to you? You couldn't do anything with it. Who put you up to it?'

'No one. It's not how it looks . . .'

'Of course not,' he said with a weary mirthless smile. 'You're only here to see Dr. Maynard, aren't you?'

'I could ask you the same question.'

'What?'

'What are you doing here at this time of the night?'

'Ha!' snorted Devane. 'That's the real joke. I really am here to find Dr. Maynard.'

'What for?'

'To warn him'

'About what?' asked Stephen.

'It's not only me who's in hot water over this whole wretched business. The powers that be are creating merry hell about there being nothing in the general hospital notes about Eileen Whatever's-her-name having AIDS. One scapegoat isn't enough. They want Maynard's head as well.'

'I know you don't believe me, but I really was expecting to meet him here twenty minutes ago. I'm sure he won't be long.'

Dr. Devane made no direct response to Stephen's statement. He turned and placed the palm of his hand on the "category 3 pathogen room" door.

'So you think Maynard's got the tissue cultures in there, do you, Dr. Hobbs? I suppose you could be right. I'm beginning to believe people in this hospital are capable of just about anything. I'll leave him to sort his own mess.'

With this Devane walked out of the lab and down the corridor and stairs. Before leaving the building he went into the records office and returned Eileen Pearce's notes. Stephen stood at the bottom of the stairs and watched his dejected figure shamble out into the darkness. Just before he opened the door Devane turned towards Stephen as though he had one more thing to say. But no words came, only a look of injured bewilderment mingled with disgust.

Although he had done nothing wrong, Stephen was left feeling guilty and partly to blame for the virologist's misery. He would have liked to justify himself, but it was clear that the man had decided he was party to a deviousness and unscrupulousness endemic among the medical staff of St. Nathaniel's and no amount of explanation could shift this view. Now that Devane had gone, Stephen went upstairs again to wait for Richard Maynard. He sat down in the men's waiting-room. He tried to read an item on herbalism in a three-year old copy of the "Reader's Digest" which was lying on a table covered with an untidy collection of ancient Sunday colour supplements and copies of "Punch". He took nothing in being unable to exorcise the disapproval of Dr. Devane. At last he heard the main door downstairs open followed by the sound of someone running up the stairs two at a time.

'Stephen, I'm terribly sorry I'm late,' panted a smiling Richard Maynard as he rushed into the waiting-room. 'I got impossibly tied up.' He walked over to Stephen and putting his arm round his shoulder led him in the direction of his consulting-room. 'What can you think of me? Come into my room and we'll get this wretched injection out of the way.'

Once inside the consulting-room Stephen sat down in the chair offered to him.

'God, I can't stand committee meetings,' said Richard as he unlocked a cupboard and removed a small cardboard packet and a syringe. 'They just go on and on and on. Boring old farts making points of order and spewing out the same old opinions and anecdotes over and over again. Two whole hours, two bloody hours, just to decide whether the students' bar should be allowed to have a cigarette vending machine. And even then no firm conclusion reached. There wasn't any time to discuss the pro's and cons of a contraceptive machine. Probably just as well. We've got that burning issue to look forward to next time we meet.'

While he was speaking, Richard opened the packet and took out a vial of powder and an ampoule of diluent fluid. He snapped the top of the ampoule and drew up its contents into the syringe before squirting it into the vial. He then mixed the powder and diluent together by shaking the vial vigorously.

'Have you still got the symptoms?' he asked as he drew up the mixture into the syringe with his back turned towards Stephen.

'Not quite as bad as at the beginning but it's still uncomfortable.'

'Well, this will soon sort you out.'

Richard turned round and put the vial down on the far end of the desk just out of Stephen's range of vision. He held the syringe up to the light and flicked it until the air bubbles gathered at the neck of the syringe. He put a new needle on and removed its guard. He then pressed the plunger lightly causing a thin jet of liquid to arc upwards.

'Just take off your white coat, could you please, Stephen?'

Stephen did as he was told and went over to the door to hang the coat on the hook. As he looked at his white coat hanging there, he remembered how Henry Price's coat had hung so neatly on the inside of the cubicle door in the lavatory in the doctors' residence. He turned back to see Richard standing with syringe at the ready.

'Just undo your belt, Stephen, and pull your trousers down a short way and we'll pop the stuff in.'

Slowly and clumsily Stephen undid his belt and pulled the waistband down three inches to reveal a small upper portion of his right buttock.

'Just a little further,' said Richard as he pulled the trousers down another three inches. He then rubbed the target area with a medicated swab. 'Stephen.'

'Yes?'

'Just why are you so interested in Henry Price?'

Stephen had had enough. He pulled up his trousers and backed quickly towards the door.

'I'm sorry,' he stammered, 'I'm just . . . I don't think . . .'

'What on earth's the matter? Surely you're not scared of injections?'

'I want to see the vial . . . and the ampoule.'

'What?' asked Richard in amazement.

'Please show me the vial and the ampoule. I must see them. Just put them back in the packet.'

'All right. Keep your hair on.'

'No. Don't bring it to me. Just push it down to this end of the desk.'

Richard did as he was asked. Stephen picked up the packet and inspected its contents. They appeared genuine but he threw them into the bin.

'That's six pounds worth down the drain,' commented Richard.

'Now throw away the syringe, please.'

'Look, Stephen, you've got to have the spectinomycin or . . .'

'Throw it away,' Stephen insisted still leaning back against the door.

'All right,' said Richard pushing the syringe into the box for used syringes. 'Would you mind telling me what this is all about?'

'Now give me the key to the cupboard.'

Stephen took the key and unlocked the cupboard. He took out some more spectinomycin.

'Would you hand me a syringe please?'

'Are you sure you wouldn't be safer if you got it yourself?' asked Richard with a sarcastic smile.

'Where are they?'

'There are some on the trolley behind me.'

Stephen put the ampoule and vial down on the desk. He then changed his mind and picked them up again.

'You think I'm going to switch them when your back is turned, do you Stephen?'

Without giving an answer Stephen walked quickly past him and selected a syringe and needle from the bottom of their respective piles on the trolley. He returned to the far end of the room and prepared the injection. He could not help blushing as he undid his belt again and pulled the waistband of his trousers down. He counted three to himself and then thrust the needle deep into the muscle of his buttock. It required a surprising amount of force to depress the plunger adequately. It was reassuringly painful. No poison would hurt like that. He withdrew the syringe and quickly pulled his trousers up and did up the belt. He walked over and placed the syringe and needle into the waste-box on the trolley behind Richard Maynard.

'Are you happy now?' asked Richard. 'Can you tell me what all that was in aid of?'

'Just a precaution.'

'What are you so paranoid about?' As Stephen made no reply he continued. 'You never answered my original question.'

'What question?'

'Come on, Stephen, you know what I'm talking about. Why are you so interested in Henry Price?'

'Why are you so interested that I'm interested?'

'So you admit that you're interested?'

Stephen decided there was no point in being evasive any longer.

'I never thought Henry's death was suicide . . .'

'Neither did I.'

'And I've never been convinced his death was entirely natural either.'

'You mean foul play?' laughed Richard. 'You have got a vivid imagination.'

'Look, I know about Henry's frozen serum from Uganda. I know he was working in the Virology Department and was propagating virus in a tumour cell culture.'

'You have been busy, haven't you?'

'I am also nearly a hundred per cent certain that he was working on AIDS. I know too that he had AIDS himself.'

'What else do you know?'

'That it's a bit of a coincidence his tissue cultures have gone missing from the Virology Department "category 3 pathogen room".'

'Now let me get this straight, Stephen. You think all this ties up with Henry's death and that I'm not entirely unconnected in some way?'

'It's a reasonable theory. You knew Henry well and presumably about his research. You knew its importance and you have the facilities to continue his work.'

'Are you seriously suggesting I had something to do with his death?'

'I don't know. But it strikes me as possible . . .'

'But, Stephen, I loved and admired the man. Not only was he a first-rate immunologist, he was my brother-in-law.'

Stephen was speechless.

'Angela Price,' continued Richard, 'is my sister.'

'Then why did she tell me not to trust you?'

'What do you mean?'

Stephen reached into his trouser pocket and produced the piece of typing paper with the words 'make sure h gets credit dont trust the others prof & r'.

'What is this?'

'Your sister typed it on her "Possum" machine the last time I visited her. Just before you returned with the two boys.'

'You think "r" refers to me?'

'Who else?'

'I don't know,' replied Richard looking genuinely puzzled and momentarily dropping his expression of mild amusement and condescension. 'I suppose you've guessed who "prof" refers to?'

'Professor Carling.'

'Good God no, Stephen. You're way off beam. What could he possibly have to do with it? Henry made absolutely sure Carling knew nothing about his work.'

'Well, he certainly knew Henry had AIDS.'

'What? That's impossible.'

'Carling is the one who told me about it. Apparently Henry had told him himself.'

'But Carling would have been the last person Henry would have talked to. He couldn't stand him.'

'Well, somehow he had found out. If "prof" doesn't refer to Carling, who else could it be?'

'Isn't it obvious?'

'Not to me.'

'Professor Hamish, of course. Who else at St. Nathaniel's would be likely to be interested in AIDS?'

Stephen told himself it really was about time he got rid of his determination to involve Carling in the whole affair. His prejudice and dislike had repeatedly led him up the wrong path and prevented him seeing the obvious.

'All right,' he said, 'I accept Hamish might have been interested in Henry's work, but what proof is there that he knew about it in the first place?'

'Of course he knew about it. Henry was a bit optimistic in thinking he could keep what he was doing secret indefinitely. Eventually Hamish got wind of it. When he realised the importance of what he was doing, he approached Henry and offered him lab space, a senior research post and even a research registrar to assist him. It was a good offer.'

'Why didn't he accept?'

'His illness had changed him. He became suspicious and even paranoid. He didn't trust Hamish. He felt sure that once he had accepted the offer, he would be gradually levered out of control of the project.'

'And the tissue cultures which have disappeared from the virology lab – what do they contain?'

'Two contain live HTLV-III and the other inactivated virus.'

'You mean he had developed a vaccine?'

'That's right. He was streets ahead of anyone else.'

To Stephen's surprise Richard began to relate the whole story of how the vaccine came into being. When Henry had returned from Uganda, he was unable to work for a year. Not because he could not find a job but because he had become deeply depressed as a result of the events leading to his departure. He was depressed at the destruction of the department he had worked so hard to build up at Makerere and became convinced that the introduction of western technology to undeveloped countries was the modern equivalent of the missions which were one of the arms of the old imperialism. But most of all he was shattered by the death of his friend Sanu, the Indian technician burnt alive by Amin's mob. He blamed himself for the death; in particular he blamed his preoccupation with his research. He felt that if he had been more aware of what was happening in Uganda, he could somehow have prevented the killing. Sanu had been about to leave for England to take up a post in a prestigious research institution but had been persuaded by Henry to delay his departure in order to help him complete some important work. The experience coloured his whole view of medicine and led him to reject immunology and return to clinical medicine.

Henry stored the specimens he managed to bring out of Uganda in a refrigerator and forgot about them. Then two years ago he realised what they might contain. First he proved that the serum contained not only HTLV-III antibody but the active virus itself. He then tried to clone the virus in bacteria but got nowhere. Instead he switched his attention to tissue cultures and after several months developed a tumour cell line which he infected with the Rigbo serum. The result was quite beyond his expectations. The virus multiplied and multiplied and he soon realised he was in possession of the largest laboratory population of HTLV-III in the world. Henry had created more than a research tool, he had created an industrial process. His unlimited supply of HTLV-III gave him endless opportunities to manipulate the virus in the attempt to inactivate or attenuate it for use as a vaccine. Irradiating the virus failed, but eventually he found a chemical means of inactivating HTLV-III, which preserved its protein coat while destroying its virulence. The first animal tests were successful. 'Is that how he developed AIDS?' asked Stephen.

'Yes. It happened about nine months ago. He never took proper precautions and infected himself by needle-stick injuries on several occasions. Four months ago he suspected that he was getting AIDS and a biopsy of a lymph gland under his arm proved it beyond doubt. Possibly being a diabetic made him more than usually vulnerable to developing the full syndrome instead of just the presence of antibodies.'

So Sally Mason had been right, thought Stephen. He was unable to understand why, but he felt relieved and heartened that Henry's AIDS had been the product of his scientific endeavours rather than his social life.

'I suppose you think I stole the tissue cultures,' said Richard.

Stephen did not reply.

'If it will put a stop to your curiosity,' Richard continued, 'I might as well tell you that I have got them and they're sitting safe and sound in our "B 1 room" fridge. I simply removed them to stop anyone else taking them, or worse still someone throwing them out.' He paused and looked at Stephen expecting a response. None came. 'Look, Stephen, when it all gets written up for the journals, you can rest assured Henry's name appears first in the list of authors.'

'I'll make sure it does,' said Stephen. 'When did you take them from the virology Department?'

'A few nights ago. Why?'

'Then you've still got some explaining to do.'

'What now, Stephen?' asked Richard wearily.

'What about Eileen?'

'Who?'

'Eileen Pearce.'

'Eileen Pearce?'

'Yes. You know the name?'

'Of course, she's one of our patients.'

'*Was* one of your patients. Haven't you heard?'

'What?'

'She was found dead this afternoon in the virology lab "B 1 room". In the lower compartment of the fridge Henry kept his tissue cultures in. Appears to have taken a heroin overdose and somehow locked herself inside the fridge.'

'Good God.'

'Henry used to look after her didn't he?'

'Yes. She was St. Nathaniel's first female AIDS patient. Henry diagnosed it himself about three months ago during one of her overnight admissions. Presumably it was the result of her drug habits. The more usual means of infection seems pretty unlikely.'

'But what can she have been doing in the virology lab round about the time you removed the cultures?' asked Stephen almost aggressively.

'You're not going to let me off the hook, are you Stephen?'

'No.'

'I don't know the answer to that. But she knew where the Virology Department was. Henry used to see her there. She only came to the clinic on one occasion and created a dreadful scene screaming abuse at other patients and the staff. She refused to let anyone talk to her, let alone examine her. She insisted she would only see Henry because he was the only doctor she trusted. In the end she became violent and we had to bleep Henry urgently. Eventually he managed to calm her down, but she refused ever to come to the clinic again.'

'Why?'

'Ha!' laughed Richard, 'that's the ironic bit. She said she wasn't a whore and the clinic was a place for whores and queers. So Henry agreed to take over her care and saw her once a week in the Virology Department.'

Stephen was not entirely convinced.

'What's that?' Richard suddenly hissed before Stephen could think of his next line of questioning.

'What's what?'

'Sssh! I thought I heard something.'

'I didn't hear anything.'

'Sssh! There it is again. Someone shutting a door.'

Richard went over to the door and opened it noiselessly. The corridor was empty. He walked without a sound down towards the lab at the end of the corridor. Stephen followed. The door to the lab was no longer slightly ajar as Stephen had left it. The two of them went in. There was still no one to be seen. They walked down to the end of the lab and there through the window in the "B 1 room" door with his back to them could be seen a white-coated figure familiar to Stephen. Richard was about to go in but changed his mind and led Stephen back to a position where they could not be seen. They heard the door open and shut again and then approaching footsteps. Stephen was hoping it wasn't who he thought it was, but when the footsteps reached where they were standing any doubt was dispelled. He now knew who was the 'r' of 'prof & r'.

'Justin,' said Stephen as he stepped forward. 'What on earth are you doing here?'

Justin was speechless.

'Professor Hamish put you up to this didn't he?' Richard stated rather than asked. 'Are you just here to spy? Or to take the cultures?'

Justin suddenly made off through the lab door. Richard pushed Stephen aside and ran after him. Halfway down the stairs he caught up and pulled Justin down. They slid to the bottom of the stairs and tumbled into the foyer. Richard clambered on top of Justin and pinned down his arms with his knees. Grabbing his lapels he began to knock the back of Justin's head repeatedly against the floor with uncontrolled violence.

'I'll bloody murder you,' Richard shouted.

Managing to overcome his astonishment, Stephen realised he had to do something before Justin was seriously hurt.

'For God's sake, you'll kill him!' he screamed.

But Richard simply carried on banging Justin's head on the floor. There was nothing else for it. Stephen went up behind Richard, threw his arms over his head and with his hands linked pulled backwards and upwards on his chin. Justin managed to wriggle free.

'I haven't got the cultures,' pleaded Justin desperately. 'I only looked at them. Look, my coat pockets are empty . . . I don't have them . . .'

Justin began to empty the contents of his white coat pockets on to the floor. An only slightly calmer Richard spoke:

'Don't give me that crap. You were going to steal them, weren't you? . . .'

'I . . . I . . .' stuttered Justin.

'You came up here for the express purpose of stealing the cultures, didn't you? . . . Didn't you? Did Professor Hamish tell you to do it?'

'Not exactly . . . Not in so many words . . .'

'Does he know you're here?'

'No. Look,' said Justin beginning to collect himself, 'You can see that I haven't taken the cultures . . . and anyway they're no longer of any use to anyone . . .'

'What do you mean?'

'They're ruined.'

'They can't be.'

'Well, they are. I'll show you.'

With Justin leading the way the three of them went back up the stairs and into the lab. They entered the 'B 1 room'. Justin pointed at the refrigerator.

'Look,' he said, 'someone has deliberately wedged open the door and the cultures have thawed.'

Inside the fridge the light, which should have come on when the door was open, had been smashed. On the top shelf lay three sealed plastic flasks. The inner walls of the fridge were lined with beads of moisture and vertical rivulets, which were beginning to form a small pool on the floor of the 'B 1 room'. Richard groaned, leant back against the wall and covered his face with his hands. Eventually he turned to Justin.

'Did you do this?'

'Of course not,' replied Justin Rugwood.

'Give me one good reason why I should believe you.'

'Give me one good reason why it should be in my interests to destroy Henry Price's tissue cultures'.

Richard appeared to be satisfied that Justin was not the culprit.

'Well,' he said, 'whoever did do it has certainly ruined everything. They've ruined bloody everything.'

'But why should anyone do such a thing?' asked Stephen.

'There's obviously someone determined to sabotage AIDS research in this hospital.'

'But who?'

'You were at the AIDS seminar, weren't you? You saw the hostility to our work.'

'But they wouldn't go this far. You're being paranoid.'

'Well, someone's done it, haven't they? I've every right to be paranoid.'

CHAPTER TEN

Stephen did not have to go into work the next day. But it was not exactly what you could call a day off and there would be little time to ruminate further over Henry Price's death. That day he was to be stripped of his identity as Dr. Stephen Hobbs and become candidate number 358 in the part two examination for Membership of the Royal College of Physicians. He had passed the written section six weeks before and was now entitled to attend the clinical exam. It would be his second attempt. As he put on his one dark suit, he pondered his lack of preparedness. Like the other candidates at St. Nathaniel's he should have been attending courses to perfect his examination technique. He should have been stalking the wards keenly and pouncing on suitable "clinical material" to practise his skills on. But even if Henry's death had never occurred, he doubted that he would have been better prepared. The truth was he had lost interest. It wasn't that he wanted to fail but that he didn't care enough to make the effort necessary to be sure of passing. His pessimism grew as he inspected his suit. Perhaps the examiners would not notice the broad lapels and flared trousers which belonged to a decade ago. Perhaps he would strike lucky and have five easy cases.

It was nearly ten in the morning and the exam was being held at St. Timothy's south of the river at eleven. He was just putting on his ancient fawn duffel coat when there was a knock on the door. It was his landlady Mrs. Patel. There was a phone call for him downstairs.

'I am sorry I am having to disturb you, Dr. Hobbs, on such an important day,' said Mrs. Patel. 'I tell him you have many important things today, but this man is saying he must talk with you.'

'That's quite all right, Mrs. Patel. I was just about to come down anyway.'

He went downstairs to the coin-operated telephone by the front door. He picked up the receiver. Mrs. Patel retreated to the kitchen and watched him from the door. In front of her stood her ten-year old son and two younger daughters. They looked at Stephen with a mixture of pride and awe.

'Hello,' said Stephen.

'Stephen, is that you? It's Justin.'

Stephen made no reply.

'Stephen, I just wanted to explain about last night.'

'What's there to explain? It all looked pretty self-explanatory to me. You don't have to make any excuses.'

'I know how it must have looked but it's not as simple as it probably seems to you . . .'

'Justin, I can't talk now. I've got to be at St. Timothy's by eleven.'

'You've got bags of time. Job interview, is it?'

'No. Membership. Remember? That exam you passed first time.'

'Oh God, yes. Of course. I forgot. I'm sorry Stephen. Anyway you're bound to pass,' Justin said rapidly. 'No, I've got to talk to you about last night. The thing is . . .'

'Look, Justin, I don't want to talk just now.'

'Then how about this evening at "The Apple and Pears"? You'll need someone to help you celebrate.'

'Commiserate with more like.'

'There's something I've got to tell you.'

'So you keep telling me.'

'No, not just about last night.'

'What then?'

'Something about Carling. I'm sure you'll be interested.'

'I've lost interest in him. I realise now he had nothing to do with it.'

'I'm not so sure.'

'What is it then?'

'I thought you were in a hurry, Stephen.'

'So that's the carrot to get me to listen to your explanation of last night?'

'If you like,' Justin said teasingly. He seemed remarkably unscathed by the previous night's events.

'Okay. I'll see you at half past six.'

Stephen put the receiver down and turned to open the front door. The children ran towards him shouting 'Good luck Dr. Hobbs! Good luck, Dr. Hobbs!'

'You'll pass this time. I know you will,' said the ten-year old boy earnestly. 'My uncle says nearly everyone fails the first time. He took four goes to pass and now he's a consultant.'

'I hope you're right,' Stephen smiled.

'I'm going to be a doctor too when I grow up.'

There was a steadfastness in the boy's large brown eyes which made Stephen sure he would achieve his ambition.

'I'm sure you'll make a better job of it than me, Azad.'

Stephen stepped out from the curry warmth of the house into the cold February air. He was not so concerned about letting himself down. He minded more about disappointing the Patels. And, of course, his parents. He was the first person in his family ever to get a university education. His sister had married at eighteen, divorced at twenty-five and now worked as a part-time hairdresser. His brother had played fourth division football for a few years and now had a clerical job in the local social security office. His parents would do their best to conceal their disappointment when he failed again. If only they didn't care so much, thought Stephen, it would be much easier.

It had snowed overnight and the pavement were awash with melting slush. He never usually bothered about his shoes. But today he had taken the trouble to borrow Mr. Patel's polish and brush and actually clean them. They had come up quite well, but already their shine was splattered by exclamation marks of dirty grey-brown slush. His flapping flares did not escape either. Soon they too were streaked with the top-soil of Stoke Newington's pavements. On the tube train down to St. Timothy's he set about wiping his shoes clean on the calves of his trousers and cuffing his shins with his hands. Next to him a couple of aggressive-looking sixteen year olds were ignoring the no smoking signs and blowing clouds of smoke in his direction. About the worst thing you could do at a clinical exam was to turn up reeking of stale cigarettes. At the next stop he jumped off and changed to another carriage. As inconspicuously as he could, he sniffed his shoulders, arms and collar to see how tenaciously the fug of the previous carriage had clung to him. Next he turned his attention to his fingernails. They had been perfectly clean when he left, but travelling on London Transport had changed all that. He should have cut them shorter. The white crescent of excess nail only served to exaggerate the line of grime that had appeared under each one of them. He tried to use the nails of the middle and index fingers to excavate under the nails of the other hand but succeeded only in wedging the grime in more deeply. The next resort was to teeth. Starting with the left thumb he placed the nail between an incisor and canine. Slowly he pulled the nail through the narrow gap. All went well until the end became jammed allowing no movement in either direction. There was no option. Stephen yanked his thumb free leaving a corner of the nailbed tender, red and exposed and a splinter of nail uncomfortably lodged between the teeth. By the time he reached his stop he had managed to remove most of the splinter, but a small fragment stayed behind and nagged tiresomely.

Although St. Timothy's was a mediaeval foundation, its main building was an early 1970's award-winning stack of glass and concrete. One wing was under scaffold and closed for repairs. At the enquiry desk Stephen asked where the exam was taking place and was directed to the fourth floor. The lift took him to a reception area where a dozen suited young doctors sat on low-backed armchairs with orange upholstery or paced on the dark-blue rope carpet. He was quarter of an hour early, and he was not surprised that his number was not among those read out by the invigilator when the next batch of examinees were called in. Clinical exams always ran late. He sat down and fiddled with his stethoscope. Should he put it in his jacket pocket? No. Too bulky and too scruffy. Should he hang it round his neck? No. Either too cocky or too keen. Best simply to carry it curled up in one hand. At eleven he watched the hands on the clock on the wall opposite pass his allotted starting time. Another quarter of an hour passed and new candidates arrived. The invigilator returned and Stephen jumped to his feet. Candidate numbers 54 to 59 were called. A wave of nausea rose in his stomach. For the fifth time that morning he pulled out the letter from the Royal College of Physicians and checked it. The time was right, the date was right and so was the place. They couldn't possible be running that late. He hurried over to the invigilator.

'Excuse me. My number's 358 and I've been here half an hour.'

The invigilator turned over the sheets on his clip-board scanning the columns of numbers.

'I'm sorry. We don't seem to have a number 358. Are you sure you've got the right day?'

'Here. Look,' said Stephen thrusting forward his letter. The invigilator looked puzzled, scanned the letter a couple of times and turned it round to look at the back as if checking a possible forged banknote. Finally he spoke.

'But this isn't the Membership Exam. This is Ophthalmogy Fellowship. Try the eighth floor. But I'm not absolutely sure.'

Without waiting to retrieve the letter, Stephen rushed to the lifts and banged the "up" button.

'Come on, come on you bloody lift!' he hissed through clenched teeth.

When the lift eventually stopped and opened, it contained a porter with a food trolley and two patients in wheelchairs each accompanied by a nurse, none of whom wanted to get off or make room for him. Stephen made for the stairs and sprinted up two steps at a time.

'Shit! Shit! Shit! Shit!' he swore rhythmically each time his foot landed on a new step. 'Shit! Shit! Shit! Shit!'

No examiner, however sympathetic, could pass a candidate who was twenty minutes late. Completing his twenty-fourth 'Shit!', he burst through some swing-doors into the eighth-floor reception area to hear the number 358 called out. He thanked God a thousand times and promised to be a better person in the future. Panting for breath he followed the invigilator into the examination area. He began to realise how badly he did want to pass the exam and cursed his stupidity in not having done enough preparation.

The first part of the clinical exam was the "long case". He was allowed forty-five minutes with the patient and was expected to take a full history and make a full examination before discussing his findings with the examiner. He was in luck. The only problem with his long case was the patient's Glaswegian accent, lack of teeth and a speech defect caused by a small stroke. Apart from that he couldn't have wished for an easier case. Mr. James Gray was a veteran of numerous finals and Membership exams. It was an easy way to earn a few quid, and he loved talking about his ailments to a captive audience. He told Stephen everything he should know, including his several diagnoses, and made sure he elicited all the physical signs. He was also fortunate in his first examiner, a benign old physician from Birmingham who had the encouraging habit of nodding repeatedly during the discussion of the long case. He was then led by the second examiner, a younger physician from St. Timothy's itself, to a four-bedded ward. Here Stephen was to face the "short cases", in which he would be observed examining particular features of each patient. The first patient was seated behind curtains in a darkened corner of the room.

'Please examine this patient's retinae,' said the examiner handing him an ophthalmoscope. Stephen remembered having it dinned into him that you would fail Membership, if you did not first view the eyes from three feet away before closing in to look at the back of the eye in detail. This was to make sure the "red reflex" was present – in other words that the line of view was not interrupted by disease in front of the retina. He placed the ophthalmoscope to his eye and leant slightly backwards to make sure the examiner recognised he was looking for the red reflex first.

'What are you standing back there for?' asked the examiner sharply. 'I said please examine the retinae.'

His confidence shaken Stephen closed in and scanned the back of the eye. Fortunately he had seen a similar eye before and recognised the appearances of choroidoretinitits. He also managed to list the possible causes. He was taken on to the second patient who was lying in bed behind a screen. The examiner introduced her and asked for the abdomen to be examined. Stephen had always been taught that, in examining the abdomen, the hands and eyes should be inspected first as both could provide pointers to disease inside the abdomen. He looked at both eyes and then the hands. Again he was interrupted.

'If I want you to examine the patient's eyes and hands, I will ask you to do so. Just tell me what you find in the abdomen.'

Stephen resisted the impulse to tell the man to go and **** himself, and went through the ritual of inspection, palpation, percussion and auscultation. In the upper left side of the abdomen his fingers felt the edge of an enlarged spleen and he listed the possible causes. The third short case was also in bed behind a screen. Stephen was beginning to resign himself to the examiner being irritated by whatever he did, and like a driving test it was not the kind of exam in which you could ask for clarification or argue. He was told to examine the cardiovascular system and was relieved to be left on his own while the examiner walked off to discuss something with his colleague. When he had finished, he stepped out from behind the screen.

'Well? What did you find?'

'The patient has atrial fibrillation due to mixed mitral valve disease with the murmurs of both mitral stenosis and incompetence present. She also . . .'

'What about the peripheral pulses?'

Stephen was taken aback. No one ever asked about peripheral pulses in clinical exams.

'The radial pulses show atrial fibrillation . . .'

'You've already said that.'

'The radial pulses are of equal and reasonable volume . . .'

'What do you mean by reasonable?'

'Adequate.'

'Adequate for what? Lying in bed or running in a marathon? Come on, you should have all this off pat. Tell me about the peripheral pulses in the leg.'

'They're normal,' he said in panic rather than an attempt to lie.

As soon he had blurted out his answer, he knew he was sunk. He didn't yet know why, but the examiner's face told him so. It would have been safer to own up to the truth that he didn't know what the leg pulses were like because he hadn't felt them.

'Right,' said the examiner leading him back behind the screen, 'Let's go and look at this lady's peripheral pulses. Show me how you examine the arterial system in the leg.'

Stephen drew back the bed-cover and immediately recognised the full enormity of what he had said. The woman had no legs; both had been amputated at the level of the mid-thigh.

'Thankyou, Mrs. Deacon,' the examiner said to the patient before walking away.

Stephen reflexly echoed the 'thankyou' and pulled the bed-cover back into its original position as neatly as his trembling hands would allow. On the other side of the screen the examiner was talking to his colleague with his back facing towards Stephen. Even after half a minute, he showed no signs of turning round. Unsure whether he should stay or go, Stephen edged slowly towards the uncompromising pin-stripe back. Eventually the man turned round only to appear surprised he was still there. He momentarily fixed Stephen by the eye and with a sideways flick of his head showed him the door.

It wouldn't have been quite so bad, if he could have left St. Timothy's immediately and downed a couple of pints and a steak and kidney pie and beans. But the exam was not over. At two he had to sit a viva voce examination. He knew his gaffe meant it was impossible for him to pass, but not to turn up for the oral would create an even worse impression. He found the St. Timothy's canteen and sought temporary consolation in a plate of unidentified fish and chips with extra large helpings of tartare sauce and tomato ketchup; he was pleasantly impressed – there were still some things you could rely on in this world. He debated whether he would ever sit the exam again. One hundred and twenty pounds was a large sum to pay in order to keep the Royal College of Physicians in port and be humiliated in return. Perhaps he would go abroad – to the Turk and Caicos Islands, the Solomons or Papua and New Guinea. Or he could become a medical journalist and tell the world where and how the whole medical enterprise was going wrong, starting with the unfairness of the examination of Membership as the passport to professional preferment. After lunch he bought a copy of "The Times" from the hospital shop and browsed through it until a quarter to two when he made his way to the Conference Room for his viva.

The viva went surprisingly well. He had nothing to lose and did not care what he said. There were two new examiners. The first asked him about the non-joint manifestations of joint disease and the role of lymphocytes in various forms of cancer. The second obviously regarded the whole business as a complete farce. His look of boredom lifted when he found Stephen was able to discuss the likely diagnoses of Richard III's deformities (polio), the Fat Boy in "Pickwick Papers" (primary alveolar hypoventilation), the Mad Hatter (mercury poisoning), and the probable cause of Mozart's death (bacterial endocarditis).

Stephen emerged from St. Timothy's dazed but with some of his self-esteem restored. The big question now was how to spend the rest of the afternoon until his meeting with Justin. About the only thing he felt he could cope with was the cinema. He took the tube to Islington and was just in time for the first showing of "Le Métier des Vaches" at the "Forum" cinema. Surely both Gwynneth and Sally could not be wrong, and if he were going to see more of Sally, he had better grow to like French films. The "Forum" was almost empty and it was not hard to find a row to himself. For the first half an hour he made a real effort, but the film's main purpose seemed an attempt to be as disjointed and obscure as possible. Eventually he could survive no more and sleep engulfed him. A while later he woke for several minutes and tried to involve himself in the film again, but was distracted by someone coming to sit five seats away from him. He fell asleep again. When he next awoke, he became aware of someone sitting immediately on his left. He fought hard not to look round and kept staring straight ahead at the screen. A few minutes passed and he felt a light touch on his arm. He turned. Facing him was a nervous man in his mid-twenties dressed in a smart conventional dark overcoat and a crested club or college tie. The man fumbled in his coat pocket, held out a cigarette packet and tried to smile casually.

'I don't smoke and this is a non-smoking cinema,' said Stephen getting up and leaving still in ignorance of the inner core of meaning of "Le Métier des Vaches". His initial anger and embarrassment at having been singled out gave way to sorrow and guilt. He felt sorry for the man that he had to proposition in cinemas. He felt guilty for reacting the way he did. He didn't like being unpleasant to people and the man was hardly threatening. It was nearly five o'clock and there was still time to kill. Anything would be better than being picked up in the "Forum" cinema – even St. Nathaniel's and Paul Goss asking how he had got on in the Membership exam. So like a homing pigeon bored of playing truant he caught a bus back to the hospital.

*　　*　　*

After his unplanned meeting with Stephen the night before, Dr. Devane returned to the quiet tree-lined road in Palmers Green where he had lived for the past twenty years. His Edwardian semi had never been the same since the youngest of his three children had left home for university. Recently he had been finding it increasingly difficult to talk to his wife. She was always worrying about him. Often he caught her studying him as though on the lookout for some sign of impending breakdown. This irritated him intensely and the only way he could avoid losing his temper – something he wanted to avoid inflicting on her at all costs – was to stay late at work, withdraw into himself and evade all but the most superficial of conversations. But this night was different. The events of the day made him long to get home to the warmth and sanctuary of 3 Upton Grove. They had made him realise again how much he needed her and loved her. Now that he really had something to worry about, he would talk to her and she would be able to help. She was the only person close to him.

But as soon as he turned into Upton Grove he realised something was wrong. His parking space outside number 3 was occupied by a transit van. It must have been two years since he had last been unable to park outside his house. He drove past and parked further up the road. When he got out of the car he saw there was a group of about ten men huddled outside his house stamping their feet and rubbing their hands to ward off the cold. Some of them held cameras and some handed round cans of beer. One was repeatedly pressing the bellpush by the front door and then stepping back to look up at the windows of the upper floors of the house. Devane had already heard a short item on the radio news giving a bizarre version of the day's events at St. Nathaniel's. He had been astonished how quickly the press had got hold of the story. Obviously someone at the hospital had blabbed. But it had not occurred to him that his house might be besieged. His longing for a quiet evening vanished. His heart sank and he thought about turning round and running away before he was spotted. But where else was there to go? And why the hell should he be prevented from going into his house by a bunch of beer-swilling yobboes from the press? He set a defiant course towards his front door. The first reporter to see him tossed his beer-can into the front garden and launched his sagging round-shouldered frame to meet him. From the top of the transit van a seeringly bright light snapped on and encapsulated Devane in an unnatural glow.

'Dr. Devane,' the reporter began, 'did you know the AIDS patient found in the laboratory fridge? Did you know she was being seen regularly in the lab . . .'

'I have nothing to say,' Devane replied sidestepping the reporter and finding himself confronted by his colleagues. 'The hospital has made an official statement and I have nothing to add. Please refer all enquiries to the hospital administration.'

He broke into a near-run in order to outflank them but found his way to the front door blocked by two photographers who began to flash away. He turned away only to find himself dazzled by a new light from the top of the van. He was surrounded with no means of escape.

'Dr. Devane, you are the consultant with responsibility for the laboratory where the AIDS suicide was found today?'

'I have told you already. I have nothing to say.'

The question was repeated.

'You obviously know I am, so why ask? Please let me get through. All I want to do is get into my own house. Please let me through, will you?'

But he could not move in any direction.

'Dr. Devane, how could it happen that in a well-known hospital a drug addict with AIDS found her way into a fridge in the room where the most deadly viruses are kept?'

'All enquiries should be addressed to the hospital . . .'

'Dr. Devane, is it true that AIDS specimens were kept in that fridge? If so, shouldn't security have been sufficent to prevent entry by unauthorised personnel? . . . Is it true that four British airline stewards have died in St. Nathaniel's in the last year from AIDS? . . .'

'How many times do I have to repeat that I have absolutely nothing to say? You have no right to prevent me entering my own home. I demand to be let through immediately. You can't stop me.'

But they could and they did stop him. The questions kept coming, not in any orderly sequence but in a muddled, accusing and importunate flood. Devane felt himself losing control and his temper rising at the mounting verbal and physical buffeting. He had had enough.

'Shut up!' he screamed making a wild swipe in the air with his ancient British Airways travel-bag. 'For God's sake, shut up!'

It worked. An uneasy silence reigned.

'All right,' continued Devane, 'I'll say something. I'll give you a statement if you'll just keep quiet and let me into my house.'

The flood of questions resumed.

'Shut up!' he yelled again and a semblance of quiet returned. 'I'll say something if it'll keep you happy. You people always want a scapegoat and I'll give you one. Just stand back and give me some space. Thankyou. Is that thing on?' he pointed at the video camera and the cameraman nodded. He took a step forward and fixed the lens with his eye. 'Right, I'll give you my statement and it's all I'm going to give. An extraordinary tragedy happened today at St. Nathaniel's, a tragedy that has never happened before and will never happen again. It should not have happened but it did. No one could have predicted it. As consultant in charge of the Virology Department I acknowledge my responsibility, not for what happened, but for the fact that it chose to happen in my laboratory. I can make no excuses for the fact that the victim of the tragedy found her way into a part of the department which should have been secure. Security was lax and I am to blame for that and no one else. Well, that's it. That's my statement. Are you satisfied? Are you happy now?'

Devane turned and as quickly as he could unlocked his front door and went into his house. He slammed the door shut and bolted it. His wife was in the hall talking on the telephone. She turned her bewildered and harrassed face towards him. Her normally tidy swept-back grey hair had a wild appearance; several strands had escaped from their moorings and stuck out sideways in undisciplined mutiny. One hand held the telephone receiver and the fingers of the other were twisting and tugging at the reins of the glasses that hung around her neck.

'John,' she said, 'what's happening? People have been on the phone all evening wanting to speak to you. They won't stop ringing.'

Devane took the receiver from her and crashed it down. He put his arms around her and smoothed down the wayward strands of hair.

'Margaret,' he began to explain, 'something's happened at the hospital . . .'

'What? Tell me what's happened?'

'I'm in a spot of trouble . . .'

Before he could get any further the telephone rang again. He stood staring at it letting it ring about ten times. Instead of picking it up, he suddenly got down on all fours and yanked the flex out from the wall.

'John, what are you doing? You could have just left it off the hook.'

The doorbell began to sound. There was a short ring at first and then a series of longer regular rings. Unexpectedly the ringing stopped, but the respite was short-lived. Ten seconds later it started again, this time a continuous, insistent ring. Through the frosted glass of the front door they could just make out a heavy figure pressing relentlessly on the bellpush in the lit porch. Devane turned off the porch light but the sound continued. He hurried down the hall to the kitchen.

'John, what are you going to do?' asked his wife nervously.

She followed him into the kitchen and found him rummaging in a drawer. He raised a carving-knife and rushed back to the hall. Standing on a chair he reached up with the knife and started to saw at a wire running beneath the picture rail. The ringing stopped. The peace was wonderful; he began to be able to think again. Switching off the hall light he swept his wife into the sitting-room and closed the door. He sat her down and told her everything that had happened that day.

'Oh John, you mustn't blame yourself. It could have happened to anyone.'

'But it didn't happen to anyone. It happened to me. There's just one thing I want you to do for me.'

'What is it?'

'Leave the house. Just get away. Go and stay somewhere for a night or two. Somewhere where they can't pester you.'

'But why? Why should I be driven out of my own home? I'm damned if I'm going to go.'

'Please, Margaret, you must go.'

'Why?'

'I'm the cause of all this and I must deal with it myself.'

'But where can I go?'

'Anywhere. Joan's or your sister's. Anywhere. It doesn't matter. Even a hotel if necessary.'

'I'm not going.'

'Please, Margaret . . .'

'You remind me of how you were that Christmas. You worry me when you're like this.'

'But Margaret, this is totally different. Nothing like then. That was a one-off thing. There's no chance of anything like that happening again.'

'I want to be here to be sure it doesn't happen again.'

'For God's sake, Margaret,' he shouted in exasperation gripping both her upper arms, 'please let me sit it out on my own. Why should you have to be involved?'

Eventually she agreed to go. Not out of choice but only because he became more and more agitated the more she resisted his wishes. She packed a few things in an overnight bag and, kissing him, left by the back door.

Devane flopped down in an armchair in the sitting-room and sat staring at the fluting gas fire and the family photographs on the mantelpiece above. Every now and then he went up the stairs to the front bedroom and, without turning on the light, stood by the window and looked down on the chatting and joking reporters in his tiny front garden. There were more of them now. With the reinforcements had come new provisions in the form of fish and chips and more cans of beer. What did they know about responsibility? What did they know about anything? But contempt afforded him no gratification. It was mingled with the realisation of his own blame. He *was* in the wrong. The security in the Virology Department had been shown to be woefully inadequate and he had been shown up as someone who didn't even know what was going on in his own lab. Downstairs again, he paced round the sitting-room trying to think of any way he could be absolved from blame. There was none. He paused by the bookshelf which contained not his favourite books but those he considered the most important. He pulled out the King James Bible. If only he could find comfort there. He remembered his student days when for five years he tried to convince himself he had faith. He would have liked to be able to pray, but was prevented by the thought that it was wrong and worthless to take up prayer only at a time of personal crisis.

It was ten o'clock and just as he did every evening he turned on the television for the news. He watched the first quarter of an hour without taking anything in; the political rows, disasters and crimes washed over him. He took a moment or two to realise that the first item of the second half was about someone called Dr. Devane. He watched as though it had nothing to do with him.He saw a haggard man of sixty refuse to answer any questions; the man appeared shambling, shifty and petulant. Above all he appeared guilty. His admission of responsibility was not included; presumably it had been consigned to an editor's dustbin. His years of devotion to his subject and his honourable contribution to research counted for nothing. He had acquired more fame – or notoriety – in two minutes than in the whole thirty-five years of his working life. He poured himself a malt whisky and lit one of the cigars he kept for Christmas and special occasions. He sat down and smiled ironically to himself. I know what I'll do, he thought, I know what I'll do.

*   *   *

The press had been busy at St. Nathaniel's too. When Stephen got back there, he found Paul Goss writing up some notes on Ward 3A.

'How did you get on?' asked Paul.

'Terribly,' Stephen replied. 'I made a complete cock-up of the short cases.'

'That's what people usually fail on, isn't it?'

Stephen tried to ignore the smug smile on the houseman's slack pallid face. Just you wait, my son, he tried to console himself, you'll find out what it's like one day.

'Anyway,' Paul continued, 'if it's any consolation, you picked a bloody good day not to be around. The press have been nosing around having a field day on Eileen Pearce. Apparently, not only did she kill herself, she had AIDS. The papers are loving every minute of it. You can imagine – "Teenage Female Gay Plague Victim Dead in Hospital Danger Lab Fridge". You were lucky you weren't here. A couple of the bums and tits rags have been ringing the ward all day wanting to talk to you. I shouldn't put your white coat on if I were you. It wouldn't surprise me if there are still some reporters hanging around. Sally Mason had to get one thrown off the ward. He posed as a visitor and started to pump the patients for personal reminiscences of Eileen.'

'Is that all they were asking about?'

'That's all. Even they felt there was enough meat in the story not to go looking for anything else. Anyway, as I was saying, when Sally asked this bloke to leave, he asked her to pose for a photograph standing by the bed Eileen had been in. And when she refused, he said "Why not lend us a nurse's uniform and I'll get one of our girls to do it?".'

Paul thought it was all a huge joke. He had obviously had as much of a field day as the gentlemen of the press.

'What really beats me,' he finally concluded, 'is the thought of all those blood specimens people have been taking from her without knowing she had AIDS. I suppose it explains why she always refused to take her clothes off and allow herself to be examined.'

Eventually Stephen managed to divert Paul's attention for long enough to sort out any extant problems on the ward. Half an hour later Stephen left for "The Apple and Pears", and Paul went to the canteen in search of someone else to listen to his tales of the press.

On the increasingly rare occasions they met for a drink, Justin was always late. There was always something pressing that needed finishing off in the lab. But today, to Stephen's surprise, he was already there sitting alone with what looked like his second drink in front of him. His expression was unusually morose and he did not notice his friend come in.

'Justin, what will you have?' asked Stephen rousing him from his sullen reverie.

'Ah Stephen. No, let me get it.'

Justin drained the rest of his pint and went to the bar and bought himself and Stephen another two pints of bitter. They sat down opposite each other. They both stared at their beer. Stephen took a large mouthful.

'Cheers, Justin. I really needed that.'

'How did it go?' asked Justin mechanically.

'Terrible.'

'Don't worry. I'm sure you've passed.'

'I won't bore you with the details, but I know for sure I've failed. I made absolutely sure they couldn't pass me.'

Justin was not listening. He continued to study his beer while Stephen used the edge of a beer-mat to make elaborate patterns of spilt beer on the table-top.

'Ready to talk about it?' asked Stephen.

'The whole thing's a bloody disaster.'

'Why did you do it, Justin? Why? It was totally unnecessary. Your career was all mapped out. You didn't need to cheat.'

'It may have looked as though I'd got my future all wrapped up, but it wasn't as simple as that. Hamish was never impressed by anything I did. He was always talking about the curse of mediocrity and implied that if I didn't get a good project going soon, there wouldn't be anything for me when my contract expired.'

'Isn't that just his way of getting the best out of people? I thought you were his blue-eyed boy.'

'Hamish doesn't have blue-eyed boys . . . or girls for that matter. With him you're only as good as your last piece of research. His attitude to me changed from indifference to disapproval about four months ago . . .'

'About the time he tried to take over Henry Price's research?' interrupted Stephen.

'How do you know about that?'

'Does it matter?'

'What else do you know?'

'I know that Henry turned the offer down.'

'Yes. And for some reason Hamish blamed me. Originally I was to be a research registrar helping Henry with his vaccine. I was part of the offer. It would have meant proper facilities for him and a fantastic opportunity for me. I don't know quite why but Hamish thought I was the cause of Henry's refusal to play ball. He was furious to have lost out. Nothing much had come out of the department for five years and the chance to muscle in on Henry's research seemed heaven-sent.'

'What exactly did he say to you?'

'He told me that if I wanted to stay in immunology at St. Nathaniel's I'd better find a way of making Henry change his mind. He hinted that, if that wasn't possible, then I should try to find out exactly what he was doing.'

'And how did he expect you to do that?'

'He said how I did it didn't matter but he would prefer not to know about it.'

'So what's going to happen now?'

'What do you mean?'

'I'm talking about your future.'

'There isn't one. As from today I've been given three months' notice. I've been sacked.'

'Sacked?'

Justin sacked. The brightest student in their year sacked! Stephen could not believe it.

'Yes sacked,' confirmed Justin. 'Fired. Given the elbow. Blackballed. Cashiered. Dismissed. Maynard came and saw Hamish and told him about last night. Hamish of course acted innocent and appalled by my role in the whole sorry tale. This morning, after I had rung you, he informed me I was finished in immunology and would in the future do best to avoid all research-orientated branches of medicine. I was told that if I ever told anybody what had happened, he and Maynard would personally see to it that I never got another hospital job in Britain.'

'There's always general practice,' suggested Stephen.

'What? You must be mad. My father-in-law would go through the roof. He sees G.P.'s as the mediocrities who have fallen off the ladder.'

'Perhaps they're the people with the good sense to get off the ladder. It's getting more and more likely it'll be where I'll end up. Anyway, from his performance at the seminar the other day I'd be surprised if Percy would like a son-in-law involved in AIDS research either.'

'Ha,' Justin snorted mirthlessly, 'if he'd been born in the East End he'd be a queer-basher. To him AIDS is a disease caught by men who sodomize or are sodomized by hundreds of other men every year. They take no responsibility for their own sexual habits and then have the nerve to demand the government undertakes a crash programme to find a quick cure so that they can carry on buggering each other.'

'I always told you you'd be better off marrying outside the hospital hierarchy. I'm sorry, Justin, I shouldn't have said that,' said Stephen as he noticed his friends unusually dull eyes momentarily light up with anger. 'I'll get you another drink.'

Stephen returned with two more pints and sat down again. An awkward silence fell on them. Eventually Justin spoke.

'Stephen, I don't expect you to applaud my part in recent events. But there is one thing I had absolutely nothing to do with.'

'What's that?'

'Henry's death.'

'I never thought you did. The post mortem showed a coronary.'

'But you still have your doubts, don't you?'

'I still don't understand why, if Henry had collapsed desperately ill at the top of the stairs, he didn't stay there but crawled to the lavatory?'

'The call to stool is a common prelude to death.'

'But why drag himself to the farthest cubicle?'

'God knows. Maybe the habit of a lifetime. Some people always choose the most distant part of a public loo.'

'And then the neat way his white coat was hanging from the hook inside the cubicle. Hardly the action of someone in extremis.'

'Well, you know how pernickety and obsessional some of these queens are?'

'He wasn't a queen,' Stephen protested.

'How did he get AIDS then?'

'I happen to know for a fact that he infected himself during the course of his research.'

'Balls. Who told you that?' replied Justin, the drink beginning to make him bullish and his words slightly slurred.

'Richard Maynard.'

'Well, he would, wouldn't he? He was Henry's brother-in-law. Anyway he's an old poof himself.'

'How do you know?'

'It's obvious, isn't it? Why else should he have that stupid little earring?'

'Perhaps he just likes earrings,' said Stephen lamely.

'Crap! And you know it, Stephen.'

'Maybe. But Henry was married and had children. And I know someone he had an affair with.'

'A woman?'

'Of course.'

'Who?'

'I can't tell you.'

'Why should it matter so much to you that Henry Price was a screaming poof? You always like to maintain how liberal you are, so why are you trying to deny it to yourself? Because, Stephen Hobbs, you're just the same as everyone else. You don't like to think someone you liked and admired was queer. Remember that lonely hearts ad you found in his room? For all we know he probably spent his Saturday nights in Piccadilly seeing what he could pick up.'

Stephen felt like hitting Justin but somehow managed to resist rising to the bait.

'You said on the phone this morning that you had some dirt on Carling.'

Justin wound down. He seemed glad Stephen had changed the subject. He could see the atmosphere between them was getting unpleasant and he was not quite drunk enough to want a fight.

'You may be right about him. He knows more about Henry's last hours than he has let on.'

'What do you mean?' asked Stephen leaning forward across the table.

'At about one o'clock that morning I was in the television room watching

149

the late-night movie while waiting for some blood to arrive from the renal unit for cross-matching. Henry was there leafing through "The Lancet". His bleep went off. It was clear the call was from Carling and he was none too pleased about something. Henry suggested they should discuss the matter the next day. But that wasn't good enough for Carling. He insisted on coming in to the hospital straight away. They agreed to meet in the Rheumatology Department.'

'And? . . .'

'That's it. That's my piece of dirt. That's all I know.'

They had run out of things to say to each other and sat in brooding silence.

'I don't know whether it's connected,' said Justin eventually. 'But Carling and Hamish have been very matey recently. Carling's always coming up to the Immunology Department and spending long sessions closeted with Hamish in his office. Apparently, there have been several long phone calls to Switzerland . . .'

'Zürich?' asked Stephen getting interested.

'I don't know. But Hamish has gone off the idea of a vaccine against AIDS. Too long term a project. He wants something with more immediate dividends.'

'To get the Immunology Department back into the international limelight, I suppose.'

'That's right.'

'You mean something like drug treatment?'

'That's one possibility.'

'What about haloprofen?' suggested Stephen with mounting enthusiasm.

'I thought we'd buried that one.'

'Look Justin, we know haloprofen can cause a lymphopenia. Is there any way this could actually be beneficial in AIDS patients?'

Justin tilted his head to one side.

'Well, I suppose that if the lymphocyte depletion was specific to cells which can be infected by the AIDS virus, then haloprofen might be able to limit spread of the virus from cell to cell.'

'Brilliant, Justin. Brilliant. If Henry had really been working on a vaccine, he would have needed cartloads of animals, wouldn't he?'

'Which he could not have kept a secret.'

'Exactly. Perhaps his Ugandan serum and the vaccine were just a smoke-screen and what he was really working on before he died was the effect of haloprofen in AIDS.'

'Certainly that would have been more feasible with the facilities at his disposal. But it's all wild speculation. Too many ifs.'

'But it makes sense,' said Stephen. 'Have you time for another one?'

'No. Better not. Fiona will be wondering where I've got to.'

'You can blame me. She always thought I was a bad influence.'

'That's not true, Stephen. It's just that she thinks . . .'

'It's all right. I'd rather not hear what she thinks.'

'Right, I'll be off then.'

Justin stood up. He lingered as though searching for something more to say. But no words came.

'Right then,' he said, 'Cheers Stephen.'

'Cheers, Justin. See you around.'

Stephen watched the familiar well-kempt figure make its way between the drinkers and out of the pub. He doubted he would ever see him around again. But the bit about Carling was a bonus. He made up his mind he had pursued the whole business so far he could not stop now. Subtlety was out. He was too exhausted and bankrupt of ideas for anything like finesse. He would simply bare the professor in his lair and challenge him. He was past caring about whether Carling would ever provide him with a reference. After a third pint he felt invulnerable. The truth must and will come out. As he was ordering his drink he pulled out from his wallet the "Time Out" advertisement ringed in red:

"OPEN-MINDED PROFESSIONAL GUY (33) seeks similar for entertainment, travel and possible ongoing friendship. Serious only. Tel. 784–6318."

He went to the telephone by the door to the saloon bar and dialled the number. It was some time before there was an answer.

'Hello?'

The voice on the other end was muffled, indistinct and somewhat cautious. The pips went and Stephen pushed in a couple of 10p pieces.

'Hello? 784–6318.'

'Hello. My name's Stephen,' he said feeling distinctly uncomfortable.

'Yes?'

'I'm ringing about your advertisement in "Time Out".'

'What about it?' The voice sounded suspicious.

'I'd like to meet you.'

'Well, I don't want to meet you. So good . . .'

'Please, please,' pleaded Stephen desperately trying to think of some way to keep the man on the line. 'I really do want to meet you and talk to you.'

'Why?'

'I thought from your advertisement . . .'

'That advertisement no longer stands. I've withdrawn it.'

'I must meet you. I'm so alone,' Stephen heard himself saying. 'I need to talk to someone. I've nowhere else to turn.'

'All right. But I'm not going anywhere with you.'

'Where shall we meet?'

'The "William and Mary" near Chalk Farm. Know it?'

'I'll find it. What time?'

'One o'clock tomorrow.'

'Right. I'll be there. How will I know you?'

'You won't. I'll look out for you.'

The line went dead. Stephen bought himself another half and sat down at the same table again with his back to the rest of the pub. Suddenly he turned round with a start – a hand had touched him on the shoulder.

'Sorry I'm late, Stephen.'

He looked up and saw the clear, beaming face of Sally Mason.

'Sit down, Sally. Let me get you a drink.'

'There's no time. If we don't go now, we won't get in.'

He had forgotten completely. This was the night they had arranged to see "Le Métier des Vaches".

CHAPTER ELEVEN

The "Forum" cinema was full. They were lucky to get seats. Tonight's audience was indistinguishable from last Friday's. There were the same earnest faces, clannishly plain and unadorned, the same shapeless jumble-sale clothes. What did they all do these people? Could they all be teachers, social workers, polytechnic lecturers, workers for Amnesty International or the media? Or were some of them lawyers, commodity brokers, merchant bankers or Lloyd's men in disguise for the evening? Sally fitted in well, correctly dressed in granny clothes. Between the lapels of her faded broad-shouldered Joan Crawford coat could be seen a purple muslin blouse with pleats. Below the hem of the coat Stephen caught sight of a pair of comfortable-looking grey corduroy trousers lapping over some desert boots. But she looked cleaner than the rest of them and the clothes went well with her long blond hair and pale Victorian looks. Stephen was still in his exam suit and was well aware that its 1970's flares and broad lapels were even more out of place here than at the Membership ordeal that morning.

Stephen was determined to stay awake and read every subtitle. In fact, there were such long gaps between each line of dialogue that following the subtitles was easy. All the same it was heavy going and his mind kept returning to Richard Maynard, Carling, Dr. Devane, Professor Hamish and Justin. The film was a depressing tale of man's inhumanity to woman and woman's eventual revenge. The plot was minimal. The early part of the film was a series of episodes of two women being emotionally and physically abused by an unshaven man who was the lover of one and the husband of the other. The two women meet and discover themselves and each other. They turn on the man and humiliate him before scattering his remains in a sewer. End of film.

'Well?' asked Sally as they left the cinema, 'what did you think?'

'Interesting,' Stephen replied.

'You didn't like it?'

'In a word, no.'

'What didn't you like about it?'

'It was tedious, pretentious and pointless.'

'That's how you find just about everything these days, isn't it?'

'How do you mean?'

'Tedious, pretentious and pointless – that's how you'd describe working at St. Nathaniel's, wouldn't you?'

They both laughed.

'Don't you feel that about the place sometimes?' asked Stephen.

'Occasionally. But *you* seem to have a permanent down on nearly everything you come into contact with.'

'There are some things I don't regard as tedious, pretentious and pointless.'

'Like what?'

'Like you.'

Stephen turned to look at her. She kept her gaze fixed at the street ahead giving nothing away. They walked on in silence. You stupid fool, Stephen, he thought, you've messed it up, haven't you?

'Where exactly do you live? ' he asked.

'Just along here. Number 32.'

They turned into a street of small but well-kept terrace houses. Stephen wondered whether to put his arm around her but decided against it. Perhaps the best moment would be directly they were inside the door. Sally took out her keys and in a couple of seconds they were standing in the hall. He was so close to her he could smell her hair. He was just about to make a move when she bent down and picked up a cat. He postponed any action.

'My part of the house is upstairs,' she said.

He followed her upstairs. She went into a minute kitchen and opened a tin for the cat.

'Do you live here alone?'

'Yes. Apart from Alexander.'

Stephen looked puzzled.

'Alexander. The cat. Would you like something to eat?'

'Thanks.'

'There's nothing much, I'm afraid. Just salami, some ham. And pasta salad.'

'That's fine, really.'

'And there's a bottle of wine in the fridge. You'll find a corkscrew on the side.'

The obvious way to the fridge was impossible to negotiate without touching Sally. He chickened out and took the long way round, but she didn't seem to notice. While she put plates and cutlery on the table, Stephen opened the bottle and poured two glasses. He took the glass over to where she was standing.

'Thanks, Stephen.'

'Sally . . .'

'I'm afraid it's only a cheap Frascati from the local booze shop.'

He could smell her hair again.

'Sally . . .'

'Yes?'

'I want to kiss you. I won't if you don't want me to.'

'I won't stop you.'

'And you won't scream rape?'

'It wouldn't do much good,' she smiled. 'No one would hear.'

The cat had jumped up into her arms again and its elliptical pupils were contracting and dilating jealously. He decided to risk it. Without laying a hand on her, he leant forward and slightly down and kissed her lightly on the lips. She released the cat and to Stephen's relief it walked across to its saucer of milk. They threw their arms around each other. He held her as though he hoped she possessed some life-giving force that could be squeezed from her pores into his.

'I think we better eat,' said Sally when they finally separated.

'Sally. I think . . .'

'Ssshh! Sit down and eat your food or it will get warm.'

They ate in silence.

'Stephen,' said Sally after a minute or two, 'will you do something for me?'

'I'll try.'

'Buy a new suit.'

'What's wrong with this one?' he replied in a tone of mock hurt.

'Everything.'

'All right. If I promise to throw this suit away first thing tomorrow, will you do something for me?'

'What?'

'Sally, can I spend the night with you?'

'Is that your usual standard of chatting up women?'

'Oh no. That's way above average.'

She laughed.

'Which film did you steal that line from, Stephen?'

'Well, at least it's more memorable than anything in "Le Métier des Vaches".'

'Bring your wine into the other room. They're showing "The Big Sleep" on the box.'

They sat down in front of the television set. Bogart had just found the first murder victim in the same room as the naked drugged blonde.

'Now this is what I call a film,' purred Stephen.

'When men were men . . .'

'And women were . . . I've never been able to complete that line.'

'Neither have I.'

*　　*　　*

Sally's alarm clock went off at half past six the next morning. She was working the early shift and she brought him a cup of tea at ten to seven just before she left for the hospital. For the first time for months Stephen felt really well. The persistent pressure over his forehead, the reluctance of his limbs to force his heavy body out of bed were gone. They had spent the night together chastely, not specifically because of his recent infection but because sex just didn't seem necessary. The last thing he remembered from the night before was nuzzling into her warm back and kissing the nape of her neck. When he had finished his tea, he jumped out of bed with an ease he had not known since before he qualified. Today he would fix Carling once and for all. He hurried back to his flat in Stoke Newington for a bath and a shave. He crumpled his suit into a plastic carrier bag and ceremoniously dumped it into the dustbin outside the front door.

'How did you get on?' asked Mrs. Patel as he was opening the front door. 'Are you now M.R.C.P.?'

'No. I'm sorry, Mrs. Patel. I've let you down again.'

'But you look so happy.'

'I've learnt to be philosophical about these things. I've learnt that there are more important things in life than Membership of the Royal College of Physicians.'

It sounded silly and trite as soon as he said it, but he didn't care. Mrs. Patel looked at him doubtfully and followed his spring-heeled progress down the road with anxious eyes.

He arrived at Ward 3A at nine o'clock.

'Good morning, Sister Mason.'

'Good morning, Stephen,' she said with a faint smile and hardly looking at him. Well, you couldn't really expect her to be all over him.

'And good morning to you, Dr. Goss.'

'What's up with you Stephen?' asked Paul Goss. 'Got Membership?'

'No, nothing like that. I won't know for certain that I've failed until next week.'

'Well, something must have happened. I've never seen you so chipper.'

'Chipper? I like that. It's a good word. Chipper.'

Instead of the usual laborious plod they breezed round the ward that morning. Stephen found to his surprise a new enthusiasm for his work, an interest he had not experienced since he was first qualified. He realised that there were things that he knew, and these things were actually useful to other people. The patients seemed to respond to his enthusiasm and he felt a rapport he'd almost forgotten. When the round was finished, he set out brimming with confidence to seek out Professor Carling. He found him in his office in the Rheumatology Department. A suitcase and a black rectangular briefcase stood on the desk.

'What is it, Stephen? I've got a plane to catch in two hours,' said Carling with a mechanical smile which failed to conceal his impatience.

'It won't take long, Professor. I just want to ask you a few things.'

'Okay. Fire away. But make it quick.'

'I think I'd better close the door.'

Stephen closed the office door. Carling's smile froze and the look of impatience gave way to irritation.

'It's about the night Henry Price died,' continued Stephen.

'Oh no. Still ferreting around, are you? I thought you'd seen sense and let that business drop.'

'I'll come straight to the point, professor. I know you were the last person to speak to him before he died.'

'Well?'

'I know you were sufficiently concerned about something to come into the hospital at one thirty in the morning in order to speak with him. I also know you were angry with him.'

'So?'

'You don't deny it then?'

'Why should I?'

'Put another way, Henry was alive and reasonably well at one o'clock. At two he was found dead in what could only be described as unusual circumstances. Between one and two he had a meeting with you – a meeting which was not exactly amicable.'

'You don't still think Henry Price was murdered, do you?' he asked with an unconvincingly casual laugh.

'I'm not sure.'

'And I'm your prime suspect?'

There was no mistaking it. Carling was squirming. Stephen actually had the man squirming.

'All right I'll tell you if you must know. Yes I did come in that night specially to see Henry. And yes I was angry. I was furious, I had just found out what he had been doing behind my back. It was outrageous. All that time he was supposed to be working for me, he was involved in research that had nothing to do with the department. He didn't even have the decency to ask my permission.'

'Presumably he thought you'd never give him permission.'

Carling ignored his comment and looked at his watch.

'Look, Stephen,' he continued. 'I've got several things I have to do . . .'

'Did you know,' interrupted Stephen surprising himself with his aggression and how it enabled him to get under the Professor's skin, 'did you know how important his research was?'

'That wasn't the point. It was the principle of the thing.'

'And that was what you came into the hospital to tell him?'

'I came to tell him that as his senior registrar contract had already expired, he would no longer be employed as from the 1st April.'

'How did he take it?'

'He told me precisely what I could do with his job. He said he couldn't give a damn anyway because he wasn't going to be around much longer. It was then he told me about the AIDS. He became uncharacteristically excited and offensive. He said how appallingly I treated both my staff and patients. Said I was in the business of making people more ill rather than less. I was finished as a serious academic and hadn't had any reasonable ideas for fifteen years. But in a way he's done me a favour. He brought it home to me how I'm stagnating at St. Nathaniel's and how I must get out.'

'You mean you're resigning?' said Stephen in amazement.

'Well, you might as well know now. I'm leaving as soon as I can. I've had enough of this bloody hospital. It's taken too much from me and given nothing back. It ruined my marriage and robbed me of my children and it's taken me twenty years to realise it.' He paused and for a moment betrayed a hint of embarrassement at how candid he had been. 'Well, I really must think about getting on my way. The roads to Heathrow are nearly always impossible this time of day.'

Carling picked up his cases. Stephen had to back out of the office in order to give him room to leave.

'Stephen,' said the Professor, 'I've been meaning to talk to you again about haloprofen. You haven't written it up yet, have you?'

'No.'

'Good. You did a good job and I wouldn't want to detract in any way from what you did . . .'

'But? . . .' said Stephen thinking this sounded more like the old Professor Carling he used to know.

'Looking at it again, I don't really feel there's enough for a paper or even a case report. By all means write to the committee of Safety of Medicines, but it's too thin for a journal to publish.'

He turned to leave. But Stephen had far from finished.

'What you really mean, Professor, is that it doesn't suit you any more to embarrass the manufacturers of haloprofen. With Professor Hamish's help you've patched up your tiff with Meissner's and it's all smiles again, isn't it?'

'What are you talking about?'

'I know what you and Professor Hamish are up to,' Stephen chanced his arm.

It worked. Carling put down his suitcases again, grabbed Stephen by the elbow and propelled him back into his office, shutting the door behind them.

'I know,' Stephen continued, 'that Henry Price had put his vaccine work on one side and turned his attention to the therapeutic effects of haloprofen in AIDS using himself and Eileen Pearce as his first guinea pigs.'

For once he felt that his guesswork was close to the truth. Carling tried to force a smile.

'You really are full of surprises, aren't you, Stephen?'

'You don't deny it then?'

Carling said nothing, but tried to stare him into faltering.

'Very soon after Henry's death you and Hamish found out what he had been doing. It was just what you had both been longing for – the perfect opportunity for both of you to bolster your sagging academic reputations: you with your connections with the manufacturers and Hamish with his immunology research facilities. But was it really necessary to destroy Henry's tissue cultures in Richard Maynard's lab?'

'Now you definitely are going too far, Stephen,' said Carling looking genuinely surprised. 'I didn't even know that such a thing had happened.'

Stephen believed him.

'Look, Stephen, I really have to go now. I'll be in Zürich until the end of next week. There'll be a locum senior registrar coming tomorrow. So if there are any problems, take them to him.'

'What's his name?'

'Oh . . . I can't remember. The medical staffing office have it all in hand.'

And with that Carling finally left for Heathrow.

*　　*　　*

The self-confidence, which had stood him in such good stead in his confrontation with Carling, had deserted him by the time he got to the "William and Mary" in Chalk Farm. He had only once before stepped inside a gay pub. On that occasion it had been by mistake and he had been in the company of several medical students including two women. The mistake had been the cause of much hilarity. This time he was alone and he was there deliberately. From the outside the pub was unremarkable, and inside the atmosphere was tired and subdued in contrast to the camp vibrancy of the pub he and his friends had entered in error. It was not crowded and the few customers present looked at him fleetingly without any sign of interest. Probably it was more of an evening than a lunch-time pub, thought Stephen. He looked round as nonchalantly as he could but could see no one who fitted the description of "open-minded professional guy (33)". He went to the bar.

'What would you like, darling?' asked a fat heavily made-up barmaid. She surveyed him through eyes screwed up against the smoke trailing upwards from the cigarette in the corner of her red gash of a mouth.

'Half a lager, please,' said Stephen.

'Anything to eat?' She turned on the lager tap and left her lipstick-stained butt to smoulder in an ashtray. 'The menu's over there.'

'Thanks.' He was glad to have something to do and read every word on the menu. 'I think I'll have the melba toast and Normandy paté, please.'

She put what was left of the cigarette back into her mouth and handed him the lager. She looked at him for a few seconds while he tried to find the right change.

'Are you Stephen?'

'Yes,' he replied wishing he had stayed at the hospital.

'He's over there in the far corner behind the partition.'

Stephen walked round to the other side of the bar, where the barmaid had motioned to with her head. At first there seemed to be no one there. He took a few more steps and there behind a partition sat a slight man in his early thirties in a dark-blue suit. He had short well-cut hair and a moustache. But the most remarkable thing about him was not his features but what had been done to them. One of his front teeth was chipped. His right cheek was a deep shiny purple and so swollen that he was unable to open his eye. On his left cheek was one long straight healing wound flanked by a few smaller wounds.

'Hello, I'm Stephen.'

'Sit down,' the man replied indistinctly. Opening his mouth to speak was obviously still painful. 'Not a pretty sight, is it?'

'I'm sorry. I didn't mean to stare.'

'Don't worry. Be my guest. Stare as much as you want.'

'How did it happen?'

'How do you think?'

'You mean someone did this to you?'

'You are quick, aren't you? Yes. He did this and more.'

He was sitting in a peculiar fashion slumped over to the right. He avoided any movement.

'Are you pleased with what you see?' He asked as agressively as he was able. 'Has it been worth the tube fare? Do you still want to talk to me?'

'Who did this to you?'

'Some freak who answered my advertisement. Some frigging freak who thinks he's got some kind of mission to beat up gays.'

'Have the police found him?'

'The police?' He laughed without amusement and had to clutch his ribs. 'I've got a family to think of. Anyway, he'd plead provocation and say he was being touched up and just went beserk. No witnesses. The perfect crime.'

'What happened?'

'You're not police, are you?' he asked in alarm. 'You don't look like it.'

'No. I'm not police.'

'What are you then? You're not gay, are you? What is it you're after?'

'I'm not quite sure myself.'

'You mean you're not sure whether you're gay or not?'

'Look,' said Stephen, 'Tell me everything you can about the man who did this to you. I think I may know who he was. He's killed already – once, possibly twice. He may do the same again.'

'I don't want to get involved. Why are you so concerned anyway? You're not even gay.'

'Please. Just tell me everything that happened. I promise not to drag you into it. Did someone called Henry Price do this to you?'

The man looked puzzled.

'About forty.' Stephen continued. 'Quite tall, thin with red hair.'

'Good God, no. Not Henry. Not his style at all. But it was just a few days after the last time I saw him. The bloke said he knew Henry. Knew him very well. Said he knew all about him and that it was through Henry that he had heard about me.'

'What was his name?' asked Stephen.

'He gave his name as Barry.'

'What happened?'

'What you can see,' the man said pointing at his face. 'This is what happened. He seemed all right to begin with. We had a few drinks and then went for an Italian meal. But when we got home he suddenly went beserk and started to hit me. And he just went on and on . . . hitting, punching, kicking, spitting . . . and he never stopped talking. More like holding forth really. Everything he said sounded as though it had been rehearsed. It was quite obvious he took pleasure in what he was doing. But he was so self-righteous about it all. It was for the good of society.'

The man began to speak freely. It seemed he needed to exorcise the experience. He had been caught in a loveless marriage and had become increasingly cut off from his children, desperate and lonely. The advertisement and been a last despairing bid to find out who he was and make contact. Putting in the telephone number had been madness. Stephen listened with mounting amazement as the details of that violent night unfolded.

*   *   *

He was fifteen minutes late for the afternoon out-patient clinic. Fortunately it had been shortened because of the Professor's absence and Henry's death. All new referrals had been cancelled but he still had twenty faithful old regulars to see. The afternoon seemed unending even though he was able to finish earlier than usual at half past five. The "Special Clinic" went on until eight on Wednesday evenings so he had enough time to make sure everything was taken care of on Ward 3A. An hour later he left the main hospital and made his way to the Department of Genito-Urinary Medicine. The clinic was extremely busy that evening, and he had to queue at the reception desk his heart pounding. He was scarcely able to suppress his excitement. After what seemed an age he reached the front of the line.

'May I have your number please?' asked the receptionist.

'My name is Dr. Hobbs. I've . . .'

'And do you have a clinic number, Dr. Hobbs?'

'No, I'm not here as a patient. I need to see Dr. Maynard urgently on a personal matter.'

'I'm not sure he's here. I thought I saw him leave in a hurry about an hour ago.'

'It's most important I see him.'

'I'll ring upstairs and find out whether he's there.'

The receptionist picked up her phone and dialled.

'Peter, is that you? . . . I've got a Dr. Hobbs who wants to talk to Richard urgently . . . Yes, I thought he had . . . I see . . . Oh dear . . . Yes, I'll tell him. Thanks.' She put the phone down. 'I'm afraid he won't be back this evening.'

'It's absolutely vital I see him today. Have you any idea where he might be?'

'He's gone to his sister's house. Dr. Farrell, her G.P., rang to say she had taken a turn for the worse.'

'Is there a phone I can use?'

'You can use mine if you like. I'll get you an outside line.'

'Thanks, but it's rather private.'

'There's a call-box fifty yards outside the building on the right.'

Stephen hurried out of the clinic to the phone box. Mercifully it was in working order and he had a 10p piece. He dialled Angela Price's number.

'Come on, come on, come on,' he said out loud while the ringing tone went on and on and on. He let it ring for three minutes before replacing the receiver. 'Shit!'

Suddenly the mention of Dr. Farrell gave him an idea. He felt an overpowering need to share what he had found out, a need to test it out on someone unbiassed to convince himself he was not going crazy. There was no one else to talk to. Justin and Gwynneth were too wrapped up in their own lives, and even Sally said she no longer wanted to talk about Henry. He flicked through the telephone directory and dialled Dr. Farrell's surgery number.

'Surgery here. Can I help you?'

'Yes. This is Dr. Stephen Hobbs of St. Nathaniel's Hospital. Would it be possible to talk to Dr. Farrell, please?'

'I'm afraid not. He's on holiday this week and won't be back until Monday. Is it about a patient?'

'Yes. Mrs. Angela Price.'

'Would you like to talk to one of the other doctors?'

'No. Are you sure Dr. Farrell isn't there?'

'Quite sure.'

'That's odd. I was told he rang the hospital a short while ago about Mrs. Price.'

'Perhaps it was one of the other doctors. If you wouldn't mind holding on a moment. I'll just check the notes and the doctors' message books.'

Stephen waited about a minute during which he had to feed another 10p piece into the coin-box. Eventually the receptionist came back on the phone.

'I'm sorry, Dr. Hobbs. But there's nothing in the message-books about Mrs. Price and nothing in her notes either. Perhaps there's been some mistake . . . Dr. Hobbs? . . . Are you still there, Dr. Hobbs?'

'Yes. I'm sorry to have troubled you. Thankyou very much. You've been very helpful. Goodbye.'

He put the receiver down and stepped into the street again. What now? His impulse was to go straight to the Price's house. But he had no idea what he would do once he got there. He went to the hospital car park to collect his purple Allegro. It started with difficulty. The car groaned and shuddered as though it was about to breathe its last. He prayed it would not let him down, tonight of all nights. With difficulty it made it up the hill from Chalk Farm and into Chiltern Crescent. He drove slowly down the road past number 17. All the lights were on and none of the curtains drawn. In the car-port stood Richard Maynard's white Audi. Stephen took his Allegro round the corner and parked it in the next street. As he walked along the slippery pavements towards the house, all the "evidence" he had accumulated began to seem so thin and circumstantial. The clear vision of the probable truth about Henry Price's and Eileen Pearce's death suddenly started to slip away from him. The pieces that an hour ago seemed to fit so well together had become unwieldy and disconnected. He arrived outside the house and saw something else that further undermined what confidence he still had in his speculations. Parked a short distance along the road was a familiar car – a red Porsche. He walked up to it and peered inside. The light from the streetlamp was just enough to tell Stephen he was not mistaken. He was able to make out Professor Carling's black combination-locked brief-case on the front passenger seat. Had he been lying about going to Zürich? Or had something important enough happened to make him change his mind?

With his thoughts in disarray Stephen arrived at the front door and hesitated for a few seconds. He looked at the windows on the second floor and thought he saw a figure hurry back from view. He had no choice now but to press the door-bell. Before he had time to speak his name into the grille, the door opened.

Inside the house all the lights were on, but the air was as cold as the street outside. Stephen touched the nearest radiator – it was stone cold. He stood still in the hall, but could not hear a sound from anywhere. All he could detect was a faint chemical smell he could not identify. He went into the sitting-room. The long dark-blue velvet curtains had been slashed and partially pulled down. The family photographs had been swept from the top of the piano onto the floor. Books were strewn all over the room. The study was much the same: the desk upended and its drawers pulled out. Files, books, medical journals, bills and receipts littered the carpet. The kitchen and dining-room had escaped relatively unscathed; a single drawer of cutlery had been pulled out and its contents spilled onto the kitchen table. When he returned to the hall, he noticed the African sculptures were missing from their alcove.

Part of him wanted to turn round and leave straight away, but something compelled him to go downstairs to the basement. With each descending step, the smell he had noticed earlier became stronger and stronger. It was paraffin. He followed the smell to a room at the back of the house, which must once have been the coal cellar. The door was slightly ajar. He pushed lightly but it would not budge. He pushed harder and the door gave way reluctantly as though there was something on the other side. He stepped into the dark room and fumbled for the lightswitch. A single forty-watt bulb gave out a feeble slightly orange aura into the windowless room. He stepped further inside. The floor was covered with old newspapers rolled into balls, cardboard boxes, anything inflammable, all sodden with paraffin. Tied to a chair in the middle of the toom and gagged with a strip of surgical tape was a figure. At first he was difficult to recognise. He was stripped to the waist and a black wig had been placed on his head. His upper eyelids had been carelessly painted green, his eye-brows pencilled over thickly with black and the corners of his eyes extended by blue and yellow like some surreal Cleopatra. The cheeks were heavily rouged. In his lap sat one of the priapic African sculptures from the hall; it leered obscenely at Stephen. The pale blue eyes desperately seeking Stephen's help belonged to Richard Maynard. Stephen was just about to release Richard when he noticed two other bodies lying in the far corner of the room with their feet and hands tied. He walked over to them. Both were unconscious but with steady pulses and respiration. One was Professor Carling and the other Professor Hamish. Stephen suddenly felt an urge to giggle. There was a mad, comical logic to the scene – everyone who had tried to muscle in on Henry's achievements was about to go up in smoke in a bizarre fusion of Jacobean and Victorian melodrama with camp overtones. He untied their hands and feet before returning to Richard. He pulled off the black wig and the gag and started to untie him.

'Just undo my hands,' said Richard. 'I'll do the rest. Go and see how Angela is. He's mad. He's upstairs somewhere. He's got a piece of cloth doused in chloroform or something. He gassed me with it.'

Stephen rushed upstairs to Angela Price's bedroom. The door was open. Unlike the other rooms nothing had been touched. He walked over to the bed. She was dead, her face drained of any colour and her eyes closed. She looked glad to be free. He pulled out the sheet of paper that was in her typewriter. On it was written 'tell the boys it doesn't hurt'. There was a slight sound from the landing outside the bedroom and then between coughs a soft voice spoke.

'Good of you to come, doctor,' it said. 'I knew you would. She's all right now. She's gone to God.'

'Hello, Reg,' Stephen replied as he turned round.

Reg Dicks stood in the doorway swaying slightly and holding on to the door-frame for support. He looked exhausted and was breathing heavily. His eyes were sunken, yellow and wide-open as if at once excited and surprised. But he expressed no surprise at seeing Stephen. In his right hand he held a crumpled piece of cloth.

'I knew God would send you just like he did with Henry Price.'

'You've been a busy boy, haven't you, Reg? Are you going to use that cloth on me too?'

'Oh no, you're here to help me. I'm too tired to do any more myself.'

'You look ill.'

'Yes,' said Reg lowering himself into an armchair, 'But the Lord's work is nearly done and you are His instrument. They've got to be stopped.'

'Who's got to be stopped from doing what?'

'They're trying to overturn the prophecy.' Reg then closed his eyes and with effort began to recite: '"And I heard a great voice out of the temple saying to the seven angels, Go your ways, and pour out the vials of the wrath of God upon the earth. And the first went, and poured out his vial upon the earth; and there fell a noisesome and grievous sore upon the men which had the mark of the beast . . ." God's will must not be tampered with.'

'You mean people with AIDS should not be helped in any way at all?' asked Stephen.

'Why should they be helped?' Reg replied. He opened his eyes to reveal the rage which still controlled and kept alive his sick body. He tore open the front of his shirt. 'Look what they cause.'

His whole trunk extending into the lower neck was dotted with nodules of plum-coloured tissue – Kaposi's sarcoma.

'And that, I suppose,' said Stephen, 'is what you call the "mark of the beast". You know, Reg, I don't buy all this religious stuff. I think you just enjoy hurting and killing people and then dress it up as being God's will. In reality it's some kind of sick sexual thing, isn't it?'

Reg appeared to consider what Stephen had said in a serious detached manner before answering.

'But don't you see? – It doesn't matter what I feel about it or what my motives are. It is all part of something much larger, something we cannot alter or avoid.'

'And you think you've got a hot-line to the Almighty?'

'You really don't understand, do you?' Reg smiled tolerantly. 'We do not always know when He has called us.'

'So tell me what really happened the night Henry Price died.'

'The first sign that God had work for me was a few months ago, when Henry Price had an axillary biopsy to determine whether he had AIDS. I was the anaesthetist. I knew then that I was chosen. What I had to do became clear to me when I found him collapsed in the doctors' residence.'

'What you said at the inquest was partly true?'

'It was all true. I just left a few bits out. He had had a coronary, but it looked as though he might survive. I dragged him to the last cubicle in the lavatory so that no one else might find him. I took off his coat and placed a syringe in his hand. I had to put the vials of insulin in the hand later, but you didn't notice. Then I closed the door from the outside.'

Stephen thought back to Henry's white coat hanging neatly on the hook inside the cubicle door and the way Reg had opened the door from the outside with a pair of forceps.

'I called switchboard for the cardiac arrest team to cover me in case anyone had seen me in the doctors' residence and went off to get a resuscitation trolley and some insulin. Either he would be dead by the time I got back or I had the means to make sure he died.'

'And then I turned up.'

'Yes . . . and then you turned up – the chosen sword of God. You were the one to finish the Lord's work.'

'How could I have been?'

'You gave him the insulin.'

'But it was dextrose I gave him.'

'The syringe contained insulin.'

Stephen threw his mind back to the resuscitation attempt. To his horror he realised it could have been just as Reg Dicks had said. Reg had given him the syringe already filled. It contained twenty millilitres: the amount of insulin would have been colossal.

'And what about Eileen Pearce? Was her death God's work too?'

'That was easy. I had gone down to the virology laboratory to find and destroy Henry Price's tissue cultures. They had already been taken by Maynard. Eileen Pearce was there lying in a heap in the corner of the lab. She was confused and had been crying. Henry Price had gone and he was the only one who helped her and cared for her. She told me about the haloprofen he had been giving her. Now that he was gone all she wanted was to die too. I simply helped her.'

'And it was you who sabotaged the fridge in Richard Maynard's lab? And you who enticed first Maynard and then the other two here?'

'Yes.'

'What makes you think I'm going to oblige this time by incinerating Maynard, Carling and Hamish?'

Before Reg could reply, Stephen turned round towards a sound in the doorway. It was Richard Maynard. He had put on a pullover and had managed to wipe off the more lurid of his make-up. Somehow Reg pulled himself out of his chair and launched himself towards him. Without difficulty Richard grabbed Reg's neck with one arm and then tried to force the cloth doused with volatile anaesthetic against his mouth. With one last desparate heave of his whole body Reg managed to rear his head backwards and sink his teeth into Richard's forearm. But Richard refused to let go and gradually the anaesthetist's sick limp frame crumpled to the floor. Stephen placed him prone in the recovery position and covered him with a blanket.

'You better get an ambulance,' he said to Richard. 'How are the other two?'

'They're all right. They're both throwing up in the garden.'

Richard picked up the telephone. When he had finished giving information to the ambulance control, he dialled again.

'Darling, is that you? . . . Yes. Something terrible's happened . . . No . . . Angela's dead . . . No, I'm fine . . . honestly . . . I'm at Chiltern Crescent . . . Come as soon as you can, darling . . . I need you with me.'

He put the phone down and started to wash his face in the basin. When he had finished, the two of them went downstairs and without talking set about tidying up the sitting-room as best they could. A few minutes later the two professors emerged from the basement dishevelled and dazed. Stephen told them everything that had happened. Threatening to reveal how the three of them had attempted to purloin Henry Price's research he forced them to agree that any publications from St. Nathaniels on AIDS should have Henry's name first among the authors. Carling and Hamish then left together in the red Porsche, both bound for Zürich.

The front door-bell went.

'That will be the ambulance,' said Stephen. 'I'll go.'

He opened the door. It was Sally Mason. They were both speechless and simply stared at each other.

'Sally!' Richard called from the hall.

She ran past Stephen and into Richard's arms. The ambulance men had also arrived and followed her through the door.

'Where's the patient, sir?' one of them asked.

'Upstairs. Second room on the right,' said Stephen without taking his eyes off Sally.

'What on earth happened, darling?' she asked Richard. 'Are you all right?'

'Someone tried to kill me.'

'Thank God, you're safe, Richard. Thank God, you're safe.'

'Don't thank God. "God" nearly killed me. Thank Stephen Hobbs.'

She walked over to Stephen and kissed him on the cheek. Then she took both his hands in her own and looked down at the ground uneasily.

'I don't know what to say, Stephen.'

'Why didn't you tell me?' Stephen asked trying to stem the tears pricking his eyes.

'I'm sorry. It was wrong. I should have told you, I know.'

'And the affair with Henry?'

'There never was any affair.'

'Then, for God's sake, why invent it?'

'Angela never knew Henry had AIDS. She never knew he was gay. Richard and I decided it was best that she never knew. That story about an affair was to put you off the scent.'

'And last night . . . What was that all about? . . . What did it mean?'

She was unable to give any answer and simply shrugged her shoulders and shook her head from side to side as if to say 'I don't know'. At least, Stephen consoled himself, there were tears in her eyes.

'But why, Sally?' Stephen persisted. 'Why . . . how could you spend the night with me?'

She hesitated and then looked up at him.

'I liked you and . . . you made me laugh.'

*   *   *

"Resus Reggie" died three weeks later with fungal pneumonia. Stephen Hobbs failed his Membership for the third time and was last heard of as a senior house officer in Obstetrics at another London teaching hospital. Justin Rugwood is doing well as a medical officer at the Department of Health and Social Security. Gwynneth Morgan holds a Medical Research Council grant and has just finished her M.D. thesis; in her spare time she lives with Owen–Hesketh–Jones. Professor Iain Hamish was awarded a C.B.E. in the New Year's Honour List. Richard Maynard returned to Baltimore and Sally Mason is still sister in charge of Ward 3A. Professor Carling left St. Nathaniel's to become medical director of Meissner of Zürich. Dr. John Devane hanged himself.